IN A STRANGE LAND

CHRIS RUFFLE

EARNSHAW
BOOKS

In a Strange Land
By Chris Ruffle

Trade Paper: 978-988-8904-56-3
Digital: 978-988-8904-55-6

FICTION

EB247

Published in Hong Kong by Earnshaw Books Ltd.

Dedicated to all aliens and ausländer

"So part we sadly in this troublous world,
To meet with joy in sweet Jerusalem."
—Henry VI Part III

Contents

1

EXILE: H

So, this is what it has all come to? A mud-baked roof in this shit-hole town in the back of beyond. My man tells me that all the doors are guarded, even my not-so-secret tunnel. I saw the Roman galley slide into the harbour earlier this afternoon. Pausias has given me up. I guess they will come for me once night falls.

Maybe it's just as well. I don't think my knees could take another northern winter; I can barely ride a horse as it is. Pausias knows and has taken to sending a litter on the rare occasions when he wants my advice. The reflection in my washbowl now frightens even me. I was never what you would call handsome, certainly not since I lost an eye. But now my greying beard and snaggle teeth reveal the effects of a long life lived hard. I was never wounded, which is quite something given the number of battles I've fought. The eye? No, that was the high mountains. An act of God. The other day, I caught the look of pity in a fine young courtier's eye. The look of fear, I am used to. Sometimes a hint of jealousy of my reputation. But that look of pity hurt.

What possible threat do the Romans still think I represent, stuck out here advising a minor prince in his local squabbles? The Romans are just so fucking persistent—forgive my Punic. I have, it is true, killed tens of thousands of Romans—in fact, there is probably no man living who has killed more. But that was 30 years ago, and I was riding at the head of a terrifying 50,000-man army of Celts and Africans. A one-eyed general riding a one-tusked elephant. I can even remember its name -"Surus". You see—my memory is not so bad. Though there are some images I would rather forget: my father drowning in front of me as we tried to force a river, dragged under by his armour; my younger brother's head on a pike, being waved by the bastard Romans as they shouted taunts across the lines.

The career of a hard-fighting general is not conducive to a happy family life. There is a wife back in Iberia. Was? Perhaps she is still alive. There are no children—not that I know of, anyway. In some ways that is a comfort. There is no constraint on what I must now do. Still, it would perhaps have been nice to see home once more before the end. "Home". Carthage. A place I left when I was nine and was called back to only in my forties. I was then, to my own surprise, elected as "Sufete"—a kind of magistrate. I did my best to shake up that corrupt bunch of blowhards known as the "Council of Elders", adding domestic enemies to my foreign ones. I survived seven years before escaping into exile ahead of a mob keen to hand me over to the Romans.

I was perhaps a little harsh in calling Libyssa a shit-hole. I have seen worse places. There's a nice view down to the sea from here, the Sea of Marmara, between the Black Sea and the Mediterranean. This small town sees a decent flow of trade. But it is nothing compared to the fine double harbour of Qrthdst, "the Cup". Since the oracle told me I would die on Libyan soil, I always had a grain of hope that somehow I would see home. Libyssa sounds so similar. I should have known there would be a cruel twist in her prediction—that's usually the way.

This is the third, and least impressive, stop in my now permanent exile. Finding countries willing to harbour Rome's most famous enemy was becoming hard. My whole usefulness seems to have been whittled down to a point to poke in Rome's eye. First it was Antiochus, self-styled "the Great", a descendant of one of Alexander's generals, who managed to cling on to a parcel of territories around Syria. That inbred little weasel loved his omens and auguries; he would put more reliance on a mess of chicken gizzards than the advice of a veteran general. But Ephesus was nice place. Despite all my experience of land armies, he had me building and captaining a fleet. His reasoning was that the shipbuilders of Tyre also spoke Punic. When his ill-advised army lost to Rome, I became one of the terms of surrender. I moved swiftly on to Armenia, where I helped King Artaxias until Roman arm-twisting became too much for him. So now here I am, a kind of terror weapon to be used against neighbouring Pergamum, an ally of Rome. A weapon whose usefulness seems to have come to an end.

The Romans were better students than these Asian kings. They learned my tactics: use infantry to pin the enemy's centre, then employ cavalry to outflank and attack from the rear. Have better intelligence than your opponent. Use the element of surprise—night attack, ambush, deception. This eagerness to learn, combined with a seemingly bottomless supply of manpower, makes them hard to beat. Destroy one army and another one sits in front of you, with generals now wise to the stratagems which doomed their predecessors.

To take me, they will need to come up the stairs and through the door in front of me. Perhaps I could kill one or two more Romans to add to the grand total? But I can now barely raise a sword above my head, so I would quickly be captured and taken back for Rome's amusement. They have called me "cruel" and a "barbarian", but I always made a point of allowing proper burial rites to those generals who fought against me. What memorial can I expect if the Romans take me? A name used by mothers to frighten children and politicians to raise taxes. No. The alchemist who sold me this ring said the poison hidden inside would act fast. The sun is setting, so now is the time to test his word. I will call my man to act as a back-up, just in case of a final Roman trick. My epitaph? Not in Punic—soon who will be left who can read it? I'll use Latin, the language of the hated victors. On a modest tomb will be inscribed "*Hannibal hic situs est.*"

2

The Last Casualty

Rumours of a ceasefire have been circulating for a while. "When will this bleeding war ever end?", is a regular topic of conversation whenever two or more soldiers warm themselves around a campfire. This time, however, the story seems to have legs. More urgency. More hope. "Kaiser Bill's on the run". Fred could see that it had started to affect men's behaviour. There was greater caution. A more meticulous checking of kit. Have I got my gas mask? Yes, it's a damned nuisance, but just in case… Trenching tool, yes. Helmet, secured. Of course, there was a limit to what you could do when, at any moment, sudden death could descend from the sky in the form of an artillery shell. Or a sniper would catch you in his sights. All the men were well used to keeping their heads down, walking hunched over even away from the front line. Hands were kept firmly in pockets when volunteers were requested. Apart from those new to the front. Or the occasional idiot, who thought himself immune to bombs and bullets.

Fred was no fresh recruit. He had his long-service medal. He had survived the mud and blood and rain for three years already. But even he found himself thinking more often of home. Of his wife and his son. At 33, he was considered old amongst his team. They called him "Old Timer", the cheeky bastards. And that was to his face. What they said behind his back was doubtless worse. His work in the slate mine outside Kendal had not been a "protected profession" so he had been amongst the first to be conscripted. He was still only "Gunner Frederick Robinson Blenkharn". The Royal Field Artillery seemed to appreciate his muscles well enough, but did not like his lip—"insubordination" they called it. Not officer material. So he still hefted shells into "A" Battery's 18 pounders.

Just because he was not in the front trenches didn't mean that there was any less bloody digging. Counter-battery fire was a constant danger, so the guns were forever being hitched up to the horse teams and dragged to a new position, which would have to be prepared—revetments to be dug and trees cut down. There were fewer German planes now, but camouflage was still necessary, and took ages to rig up. They still made fun of his accent, but he pulled his weight, and they seemed to appreciate well enough the mint cake in his parcels from home.

It was early in the day when the news came though. The kettle had barely boiled. The men were still wiping sleep from their eyes, scratching the latest lice bites, and stamping against the cold, when the major told them. The cease fire would start at 11 o'clock. The reaction was not what he expected. Yes, there was the normal sceptical exclamations of "Really?". Afterall, the sounds of war continued. It was perhaps slightly quieter than normal, but Fred had put that down to the weather—it was, once more, absolutely pissing it down. But there was no celebration. No hurrahs. Instead, a kind of collective sigh went round the group, as they cradled mugs of tea or used it to dunk that morning's hard tack. Like someone who has been sucking in his belly then lets it go, a visceral collective exhaustion was suddenly revealed. The youngest recruit asked the question on everyone's lips "So, when can we go home, Sir?"

"Not so fast, Stevenson," said the major, wiping a drip from his moustache. "There are still millions of Hun dug in to the front of us." An explosion sounded. "As you can hear. I am sure our lords and masters will still have uses for the Royal Field Artillery yet. But, if I was you, I'd start practicing your German."

"Vurst is sausage," confided Stevenson to his neighbour.

"Thank you for that valuable contribution," said the Major, turning on his heel, and leaving the dug-out, vainly pulling down his cap against the downpour. To break the silence that followed someone said, "Well, that's it then. Blighty for us."

Fred thought of his brother, Tommy. In fact, he was a step-brother. His widowed mother had remarried; Thomas was one of her new husband's first family. But he had seemed a nice chap, friendly and funny. Much younger, unattached, which is probably why he had been swept up in the enthusiasm at the war's start and gone off with his mates to volunteer for the Border Regiment. His photograph in uniform stood proudly on the mantlepiece at home. Some pointed remarks had been made about Fred's lack of patriotism before the full horror of what was happening became evident despite the careful censorship of letters from the front. Tommy had not made it. Killed at Gallipoli. Well, his body had never been found, so the official wording was "Missing in action". His step-father clung on to the hope that Tommy was somehow a prisoner of the Turks, though eye-witness accounts left precious little for this fancy to cling onto.

Despite the dire predictions of the battery's pessimists, the cease-fire did go into effect and did hold. Not that the optimists gained much succour from the dreary advance across old battlefields towards the Rhine. The battery advanced along water-logged roads through destroyed towns wrecked further by the retreating Germans. There were no cheering crowds to throw flowers at their liberators. There was still little to eat and, with the first morning frost, the team's spavined horse looked skeletal. In the 251st Brigade, to which his team was attached, many men were now down with an illness which some wit had called "Spanish Flu".

Fred found time to write back to his mother, whose latest letter had been filled with excitement at the war's end and all that it promised. He explained that his Brigade were being sent to occupy Cologne, one of three bridgeheads across the Rhine under the terms of the surrender. He was not sure when he would be demobilized, but hoped that it would be soon. Surely, if there was any delay, he would be able to get some over-due leave and, with Beatrice and Keith, they would be able to eat that roast goose dinner promised in her last letter. Maybe his leave would coincide with Christmas. Perhaps she could help him think of suitable presents for his son. Keith had doubtless grown up so much whilst he was away, he was not sure what he would like now.

Fred laid down his pen, coughed and wiped his nose. Perhaps an early night would help him to shake off this bloody cold.

My great uncle, Gunner Frederick Robinson Blenkharn, died on 21st November 1918, just 10 days after the Armistice was signed. He is buried in Cologne's Southern Cemetery. Private Thomas Blenkharn, whose body was never found, is commemorated on the Hellas Memorial in Gallipoli. His posthumous medal sits on my desk as I write these words.

3

EXILE: MRS. T

June 1940

Dear Victor Lvovich,

You will be surprised to receive this letter. I know you have had your disagreements with my husband—over Kronstadt, the War in Spain, the Fourth International. But when the time comes to tell his story, it is your help that I want. I have long admired your work, comrade, both fiction and non-fiction. Your latest "Midnight in the Century" sits in front of me now, on the desk in our new home.

My husband may be the most exiled man in history. This makes me the most exiled woman, though few have heard of Natalia Ivanova Sedova. I am the one in the background of photographs—a small woman with bobbed blond hair walking up the gangplank a few paces behind my photogenic husband, with his goatee and round tortoiseshell glasses. He had already escaped from one Siberian exile before we married, so I cannot claim ignorance of the risks. I could not have foreseen, however, the sheer variety of our places of exile. You must now be running my husband a close second. I am sending this letter to an address I have for you in Paris. Let's hope you can stay there for a while—at least long enough to receive this. I was so pleased to hear that you had been allowed to leave Orenburg and then the Soviet Union all together. I think I can still claim the most remote "internal exile", however: Alma Ata was 4,000 kilometres from Moscow and 250 kilometres from the nearest railway, which makes Orenburg positively cosmopolitan. We might as well have been on a different planet. It took seventy days for a letter from his dying daughter to reach him. He has—had—two daughters from his first marriage and two sons by ours. I mostly remember Alma Ata for the sea of red poppies and the size of the apples.

The location of my husband's pre-revolution exiles were more conventional; in London, for example, writing incendiary publications and plotting. Our post-revolution exiles, after his brief, giddy time running the world's first proletarian state, have become increasingly bizarre. We spent four years in the Prinkipo Islands in the Sea of Marmara, where the Ottomans sent their own exiles. That was quite pleasant—he wrote a lot and went fishing. There was then a fraught two years in France, where an endless stream of left-wing factions tried to recruit his name for their cause. Expelled, we then suffered those miserable years under house arrest in rural Norway. Now we have the torrid heat of Mexico City. To put up with the reason for these strange locations is that most civilized countries do not want to give house-room to a committed Marxist and author of the "Red Terror". After Churchill called him the "Ogre of Europe", we started using it as his nickname. "What would the Ogre like for breakfast this morning?"

Given the constant surveillance, persecution and loss of friends and family, he has remained remarkably resilient. Mexico City is not well provided with sea fishing, so he has taken to collecting rare cacti. He also keeps rabbits; I can see him feeding them now through the study window. I encourage his hobbies as a relief from the groaning piles of correspondence, promoting "proletarian internationalism". His writing condemns the isolationist, bureaucratic despotism of "that third-rate thug

Dzhugashvili". It is his weak spot: he always underestimated Stalin. Lev, after being Lenin's designated successor and creating the Red Army, never understood how he was so outmanoeuvred by a "mere secretary". He has never given up hope that, at some point, the proletariat will discover Stalin's errors and rise up against him. Perhaps the war in Europe will be the catalyst?

When we first came to Mexico, we stayed at the "Casa Azul" owned by painters and fellow travellers Frida Kahlo and Diego Rivera. It was kind of them, given the political risk and our chronic lack of funds. The house was full of colourful art, a big change from our usual spartan accommodation. But, when my husband fell out with Rivera, I was not sorry to leave. I was not blind to his infatuation, though what he could see in such a damaged woman with a single eyebrow remains a mystery. We have only moved a few blocks away. It is less colourful—in fact it increasingly resembles a small fort—but at least it is ours. Apart from several live-in "Trotskyites" and the police guard, of course. Our grandchild, Seva, lives with us, which is a blessing and tiny sliver of normality.

Three months ago, a gang attacked our house. Fortunately, they were not very competent. The police told us that 200 bullets were fired, but no one was hurt. Seva hid underneath his bed, clever boy. Lev was calm—the result of all his long experience of war, I suppose. Now, each morning on waking, he says "You see, they did not kill us last night" and laughs at his own joke. It seems as though Stalin finds his very survival an insult, despite our reduced circumstances and influence. Since the attack, security has been increased. But there are so many visitors coming and going, anxious to sit at the feet of "the prophet", that no system can possibly be foolproof. Lev is too generous in providing guidance to his followers, even the most hopeless. On his desk I see a piece he has edited for his secretary Sylvia's new, mountain-climbing boyfriend. It is drivel, but at least the boyfriend, called Jacson I think, was thoughtful enough to bring Seva a toy glider and a box of sweets for me. When he comes back this afternoon, I am sure that Lev will go easy on him.

We have been together nearly 40 years, so I feel no compunction in reading my husband's diary when he leaves it open on the table. A testament on the flyleaf declares "I shall die with an unshakeable faith in the communist future". But his last entry is addressed to me: "Natalia. My faithful one, my love, my victim…"

I hope all will be well, but fear I might have need for your biographical services soon. If Paris proves unsafe, you will be welcome here.

Go safely in this troubled world.

Natalia Ivanovna

4

Exile: Hung

To the respected Prince Yichun, greetings.

浮云遮月隐， 落景无树微。 西风吹山巅， 峦白覆皑皑。
皓白映面颊， 东方苍翠平。 急催回忆间， 昔日鬼斧真

There is no dust to hide the moon.
There are no trees to block the wind.
To the West jagged mountains are topped with snow
Like the white hairs which fleck my beard.
To the East a vast verdant plain
Hurries my thoughts back to the haunts of my youth.
When sun sets in the capital, it is still light here.
When summoned to speak, I should have held my tongue.

I am no Tao Yuanming, but the poem is not too bad I think? There is no one here fit to judge, just soldiers and Muslim horse herders. Hence this letter to you, my old friend and the most talented of all my students. I am pleased that this letter has survived the vicissitudes of the Imperial courier system and the censors. Was the seal broken when you received it?

As you see, I am now ensconced in my banishment on the far Northwestern borders of our Great Qing empire. This part was only conquered by our late lamented emperor Qianlong in his vigorous youth, so its few inhabitants still chafe under the constraints of our civilizing mission. Even the fort looks new, the stones unstained. The duties of a magistrate here do not occupy much of my time; so far this has mostly entailed adjudicating disputes about livestock or the aftereffects of a drinking binge. So, I practice my calligraphy. It is just a shame I never learnt to paint horses.

The food is as drab as the company. I gnaw on stringy goat and drink fermented mare's milk. As a Southerner, I most miss fresh vegetables and fruit. Oh for an orange! I should stop complaining about my banishment; I know it could have been a lot worse. I see your hand, old friend, in the commutation of my sentence of "death for extreme indecorum" to this internal exile. If so, I am eternally grateful. If, after the requisite time has passed, you could put in a good word for my recall, I would be most obliged. I do not intend to die out here in the wilderness like Boyi and Shuqi. I still have work to do, books to write.

You know that I did nothing wrong. It is the official's Confucian duty to speak out when he sees the ruler of all under heaven misled by wicked and corrupt men. I refuse to "bow like a servant in return for five pecks of grain", as they say. I know that the new emperor finally saw through the wiles of pretty-boy Heshen, who so beguiled his father. I understand Heshen was sent a silk scarf and "allowed" to commit suicide. Plenty of his clique, that feasted off the White Lotus rebellion, remain in power, however. I imagine there was much chortling amongst them when they determined to exile a scholar famous for his work on the dangers of over-population to the least inhabited part of the empire.

There is one benefit to banishment. My long winter journey to this distant outpost was taxing—I arrived here four months after departing Beijing—but at least it took me through the historic heart of civilization. My official duties have caused me to see more parts of China than most men. But I think my favourite is still old Changan, imbued as it is with so many poems and stories. It was a treat to climb the Wild Goose Pagoda again. I followed the Spirit Way out to pay my respect at the tombs of the Tang emperors. I even detoured to make a libation at the memorial to Imperial Consort Yang, strangled at the demand of disgruntled generals, leaving her lover the Emperor Xuanzong bereft until his dying day. From there, my journey took me through the faded glory of silk road towns. I have kept a diary, which I hope to publish if you can help me escape my present wilderness.

Could I impose on you to pay a visit to my wife and sons? Please let them know that I am well and miss them. I have written but not yet heard back. It was a hard decision to leave them behind in the capital, but I believe it was the correct one. I know they still face the ignominy of my banishment, but my wife would have withered out here on the frontier, and it would have done nothing for the boys' education and prospects. The weather is extreme and the boredom worse.

I would be grateful if you could send out, with your reply, a new supply of calligraphy brushes and paper. They are not to be had locally. Perhaps my next poem will be more elegant and salubrious.

Hung Liangji

Written in the 5th year of the reign of His Majesty Renzong, on the 7th day of the 5th month

5

Monkey

Dear Mr Spencer,

This is Ulysses Chen from Year 5. My mother is worried about me getting a detention from the headmaster. So I am writing to explain.

It was my favourite class since I came to the school six months ago. I come from Shanghai, with Ma. Ba has to stay in China for work, but he says he will come to see us soon. Ma was recommended your school by a friend whose daughter just got into Oxbridge University. Ba complains about the money, but Ma tells him it is not the most expensive school. That is why we rent a flat in Croydon.

I know my English is not good. Even when I use spellcheck, our class teacher, Mrs Jowell, sends my essays back with lots of corrections. There is even more mistakes if I have to write in class without a PC. But I am the best in my class at maths. Some boys ask me for help with homework, but they still tease me in the playground and call me "Chink". There are two other Chinese boys in my class, but they do not get called names. They have been in England longer, and they are taller and one is good at football. Ma does not like me playing sport, in case I break something and can't play violin. I sometimes speak in Putonghua with the other Chinese boys, but the playground monitor tells me off if he hears us "English please!". My best friend is Omari. His parents comes from the Caribbean and he supports the West Indies team. He is also in the school orchestra. He plays trumpet. So at break I often play with him. He likes the soup that my Ma makes and sends in a vacuum flask every day. She does not like me having cold drinks from the vending machine as they are not good for my stomach.

I met Omari's parents at a school concert and introduced Ma. She always comes to my concerts. She sits in the front row and waves at me. It is embarrassing. She makes sure I practise every night after I finish my homework. I wish I had more time to watch more videos like the other boys — they make fun of me when I haven't heard of something famous. My English is now better than hers so sometimes I need to help translate if people phone or call. Like our neighbour from the flat above who complains about my practising. Ma enters me into local music competitions. It is a pain but she looked so proud when I won. It was only a small cup, made to look silver, but she has put it on the mantlepiece, next to the photo of me as a baby, which is embarrassing.

For my favourite class I mentioned, Mrs. Jowell asked us to research an animal. She wrote a load of animal names up on the whiteboard, and we all got to pick one. My name comes near the start of the alphabet so there was still plenty to choose from when my turn came around. I picked monkey, my favourite animal. I was born in the Year of the Monkey. Also, I thought I could use some stuff about the Monkey King, which is a famous story in China. Others picked lions, tigers and crocodiles and such.

I found a lot about different monkey species and their habits online. I have already got used to using Google now rather than Baidu. Did you know that human and chimpanzees share 99% of DNA?! My favourite ape is the orangutang. I printed out photos including a picture of the smart but naughty Monkey King. I told Ma that there is one type of baboon which eats grass, but mostly their diet is fruit. She says I should eat more fruit. Ma often puts snacks into my satchel for break. On that morning she gave me a banana.

Mrs Jowell liked my folder on monkeys and wrote "Good work" on the front. She chose me to give a talk to the class. I was a bit nervous, but it is not worse than playing violin in front of people. They liked it when I pretended to be the Monkey King, jumped onto the desk and beat my chest. Even Mrs. Jowell laughed. She said "Perhaps we will have something a little less violent next" and picked Omari, who wrote about bush babies.

That break, the boys asked me to pretend to be the Monkey King again by swinging on the jungle bars. After that I played with Omari, jumping up and down making grunting noises, like monkeys do. Omari pretended to be a bush-baby and be scared and run away. That is when I threw my banana at him. It was only in fun, and did not hurt him. Afterwards he ate half of it.

That is when you shouted at me.

Ma was very upset when I told her the headmaster had given me a detention. She kept asking "What for?" but I really do not know. Now Ma is mad at me and complains to Ba. I know she has called the school a few times to arrange to meet you to find out what I have done, but she cannot get through. Yesterday I heard Ma talking on the mobile "Perhaps this English education is not so good after all." That is why I am writing you this letter, to show I did not mean to do anything bad. Please help. I do not want to have to move school again.

Yours

Ulysses Chen

6

Exile: IA

I agreed to this interview, but I let you know that I am recording on a tape machine here. Reporters have previously twisted my words to make a joke. I have proof. So be careful.

The place is fine, thank you. It is a Novotel. We have the top two floors. There is no swimming pool, but I go to the Intercontinental for that. I like to keep fit. I was the light-heavyweight boxing champion of East and Central Africa for several years. You should let your readers now that.

It is hard to get used to the dry climate. I had them install a humidifier in my bedroom. And a fridge. What is in it? Mostly fruit. I like oranges. The staff call me "Doctor Jaffa". No, there is no alcohol. I am, like my kind Saudi hosts, a good Muslim.

Also, there are no human organs. Ha! You see I have a sense of humour. Admit I had you going. You were imagining a story "He keeps his enemies' hearts in a fridge by the bed and eats them for breakfast". Anyway, I don't like the taste—too salty. Ha! You see, I did it again. I am a funny man.

Anyway, there is no kitchen. We eat downstairs, or at the Meridien or Sofitel. It is fine. The children are happy; they can eat all the beefburgers and pizza they want. I take them to the beach. They see more of their Pa now than they did when he was running a country.

What do I miss most? I think it is my Maserati. I had to leave it behind in Kampala. A red one. Here they have got me driving a light blue Chevrolet Caprice. It is embarrassing. Anyway, it is all only temporary. Soon my people will call me back. It was, after all, a foreign army that forced me out. Nyrere and Tanzania will come to regret their unprovoked and outrageous attack. Look what a mess they are in now. Eventually they will realize that I am the only man that can sort it out. We have special satellite communications installed to keep in touch with our friends and know what is going on.

(Muffled) Mama is downstairs. I am not sure. Please don't bother me. I am on the phone to a man from the Times of London.

I am sorry that was my son…Jaffer. (Laughs) I should not have hesitated, but when you have 43 children it is not always easy to remember. You can write that in your paper, to let your readers know that Idi Amin Dada Oumee is a potent man. No, only the youngest nine are with us. Seven wives. Or seven "official" wives as it said in your newspaper. No, only one is here. I am not that crazy.

Regrets? No. Only nostalgia. I put Uganda on the map. Who had heard of it before I took charge? Now tourists flock to see our elephants. The fabled Mountains of the Moon. The astounding Kabelega Falls.

Of course, there are always critics. I would like to see them run a poor, land-locked country with so many tribes. I am not against tribes, but against tribalism. That is the curse of Africa. I was born a Kakwa, but I never discriminated.

Yes, there were more men in the army from my home West Nile region, but that is to be expected. They are taller and stronger than the Southerners. The minimum height limit of 5′8″ was perfectly reasonable. (Laughs) You have to draw a line somewhere.

They complained, but how can you expect Asians with a

British passport to work in the best interests of the country? It was necessary to cleanse the country. I always put Uganda first. Uganda for the Ugandans. That is why the Imperialists turned against me when they eventually saw I would not bow to their demands.

Did you know that Britain once offered Uganda to the Zionists as a Jewish homeland? Can you imagine how history would have been different. It made my old friend Yasser Arafat laugh when I told him. He was best man at my wedding. The most recent one.

I once had dinner with your Queen, you know. We had a nice talk. Of course, she knew that I had helped her when I fought with the King's African Rifles against the Mau Mau criminals. She was very respectful and asked me a lot about Uganda. That was why, when Britain's economy was in such trouble in 1973, I set up the "Save Britain Fund". I also offered to help her in mediating between the Catholics and Protestants in Northern Ireland, but she did not take me up on that. As a Muslim I am neutral, but have both Catholic and Protestant relatives, so I think I could have done a good job.

Wakhweya's book? Yes, I saw it. "A State of Blood". The title was the best thing about it. It is a pack of lies. He was a Cabinet minister that I had to dismiss for incompetence and corruption, so what can you expect? When you write your article, please make sure that you get my full title correct: "Field Marshal. Doctor of Philosophy. President for Life. CBE (Conqueror of the British Empire). Victory Cross and DSO."

I need to go now, so do you have a final question? What would I still like to achieve? Well, a visit to Disneyland would be nice.

7

The Interpreter

Dear Madame Zhang,

I hope that I am not in breach of diplomatic etiquette in contacting you? I resigned from the Foreign Office some time ago. Congratulations on your new job at the Ministry of Labour; your promotion is well-deserved! Please forgive me for writing in English; I do not have much call to write in Chinese these days.

My reason for contacting you now is that, in unpacking my belongings, I came across the attached photograph. I thought you might like a copy. It shows us both, armed with our shorthand notepads and mugs of tea, at the peak of our powers. This was perhaps the most consequential meeting at which I ever interpreted.

You had the harder task. Mrs. Thatcher was a pleasure to translate for. She was used to speaking through interpreters, so avoided overly florid or complicated language. She had also visited China once before as leader of the Opposition in 1977, so knew broadly what to expect. I always found Labour politicians the hardest; they do love an idiom: "We'll cross that bridge when we come to it" or "When the shit hits the fan". They are also keen on sporting idioms: "Batting on a sticky wicket" or "A game of two halves". On this fateful occasion Mrs Thatcher was struggling with jet lag and a bad cold. But she made a decent fist of what was, in my humble opinion, a hopeless case. We interpreters are allowed to have our own view about what they are translating, it's just that we are not allowed to express it.

Interpreting for Comrade Deng must have been so difficult. Apart from being deaf in his right ear (which is why Mrs. Thatcher is sitting, against protocol, on his left) you had to deal with his Sichuan dialect. There was also all the hawking and spitting to contend with. I smile when I see both of the politicians with their trademark props. Thatcher has her hand-bag at her feet, Deng his brass spittoon. There was some talk at the embassy about whether his extensive use of it through-out the meeting was a physical necessity or merely a tactical ploy, to unsettle the visitor and buy time to formulate a reply. You are better placed than me to know, but with a habit of two packs of Panda cigarettes per day, perhaps it was more the former. Also, at this time—September 1982—simply breathing Beijing's soot-laden air was the equivalent of another pack of cigarettes. I am afraid I cannot disclose the contents of Mrs. Thatcher's bag—I do not wish to breach the official secrets act—but I am willing to say that it included a can of her favourite hair setting spray, which is what gave it heft.

In terms of vocabulary, of course, you had the easier task. I was always impressed how Communist leaders in China never tire of saying the same thing. The same stock phrases would roll out again and again, albeit in a slightly different order. In English such repetition would indicate boorishness or a mediocre education, but in China, I understand that it is a sign of adherence to the party line and the expression of a self-evident truth. Your biggest challenge was how to make Deng sound polite. I remember the meeting was afterwards described as "abrasive" which, in diplomatic language, is little short of a fist-fight.

The lease on the New Territories, signed by Ambassador

Colonel Sir Claude Maxwell MacDonald in 1898 was due to expire on July 1st 1997. Although Hong Kong Island and Kowloon were officially ceded to Great Britain in perpetuity after the Opium War, Mrs Thatcher was under no illusion that this part could be held after 1997. She had been briefed that the New Territories represent 92% of the colony's land mass and most of its reservoirs. She had also been informed that the British Garrison in Hong Kong could hold out for a maximum of 48 hours against an invasion by the People's Liberation Army. Mrs. Thatcher's trump card, she thought, would be China's desire to maintain business confidence in Hong Kong. This was to be achieved by allowing Britain a role in administration of the colony even after sovereignty reverted to China.

Deng made it very clear that, for China, sovereignty and administration are one and the same. Deng was less doctrinaire on economics than Mao, but he knew that if he accepted anything less than full control he would be held as guilty as the traitor Li Hongzhang who signed the territories away in the first place. Sovereignty over Hong Kong was more important than its prosperity. I could hear you trying to soften Deng's demands—adding "please" and "hope that" and "might".

Under this barrage, Mrs. Thatcher, to her credit, maintained her sang-froid. Her coiffure was undented (a major concern amongst my embassy colleagues ahead of the visit was whether the plug for her heated hair-curlers would fit into the sockets at the State Guesthouse). But on the way out from this bruising meeting, Mrs. Thatcher stumbled on the steps of the Great Hall of the People. I was two steps behind and too slow to catch her. This photograph was front page—a great nation humbled. The Hang Seng Index also stumbled.

That evening you probably had the better food but worse conversation: I remember Deng dined with Kim Il-sung, who has flown in from North Korea on the same day, showing where his priorities lay. Mrs. Thatcher was assigned to Premier Zhao Ziyang, a more suave conversationalist, who served sea slugs to accompany the smoked salmon we had imported. Mrs. Thatcher gave him the gift intended for Deng, a Ferranti Scholar II Chinese word processor to illustrate the white heat of Britain's technological development. I was sorry to hear what eventually happened to premier Zhao—I hope his house arrest is not too uncomfortable?

I am pleased that I did not have much of a role in the subsequent twenty-two rounds of gruelling negotiations, which one colleague described as "like wading through mud", but I remember we were both present when the agreement was signed with all due pomp in December 1984. The break-through was Deng's concept, originally conceived to address the Taiwan situation, of "one country, two systems". These are empty words, of course, but it suited both sides to pretend to believe them. Mrs. Thatcher even went so far as to describe them as "brilliant". The Basic Law would preserve Hong Kong's way of life for 50 years after the hand-over in 1997. Now retired and enjoying the delights of Tunbridge Wells, I follow developments in Hong Kong with interest. I smile at the West's indignation as China tramples over the rights set out in the Basic Law. But both sides knew that this was a fig-leaf, a temporary solution to a tricky mutual problem. We were there. And Hong Kong has not collapsed, though it perhaps lacks a little of the flare of its imperial past. The "flood of emigrants" has proven to be distinctly well-heeled emigrants; Kent's fine boarding schools have turned out to be beneficiaries.

I know from our occasional conversation at state banquets that you studied English literature and are a fan of Victorian poetry so I leave you with one of the finest:

Far-called, our navies melt away;
On dune and headland sinks the fire:
Lo, all our pomp of yesterday
Is one with Nineveh and Tyre!
Judge of the Nations, spare us yet,
Lest we forget – lest we forget!

Yours sincerely,
J.T.

8

Not from around here

"You're not from around here, are you?"

He had caught the eye of the old lady at the next table, giving her the chance to speak to him. Due to his exotic looks, he got this a lot. Theatrically he surveyed his surroundings—County Mall, the finest shopping centre which Crawley had to offer.

"No".

He moved his skinny latte to the side and smoothed out his newspaper, making it clear that the conversation was ended and he did not want further interruptions. Before he could re-focus on the report of last night's Brentford v. Arsenal game, however, an internal dialogue fired up. It's just a little, old lady in a damp raincoat. Under the table he could see an umbrella drying next to sensible, old lady shoes. She is probably lonely. Who drinks tea at Costa Coffee? She just wants to talk to someone. Be nice.

"I mean I was brought up here, but I was born in Mauritius. Originally my family comes from the Chagos Islands." At this point, the eyes of the listener normally went blank, so he had a spiel prepared. "It's a group of islands in the middle of the Indian Ocean. Thousands of miles from anywhere. The British government cleared the population out in the 1960's. Some of us ended up here, probably because it's the closest town to Gatwick Airport. We certainly didn't come here for the weather." He laughed at his own joke and looked out the window at the rain battering the car park.

She smiled: "Have you ever been?"

"To the Chagos islands? Oh no, no one is allowed there. But my Grandma talks about it all the time. Beautiful beaches. Coconut palms. Tropical paradise. That kind of thing. I guess we have always got Brighton beach."

"I lived there."

"Sorry?" He started to regret talking to this little old lady. It might be that dementia thing.

"I lived on the Chagos Islands for a couple of years. It was about twenty years ago. I served at the military base on the biggest island, Diego Garcia. I was the secretary to the "British Rep". Naval Party 1002, Sir!" She gave a mock salute, knocking the table and causing a tsunami in her teacup.

"Gosh! So, you actually guessed where I came from before you talked to me."

"Yes. In some ways I miss my time there, and it's not often I find someone to talk to about it."

"So what are you doing in Crawley?"

"Oh, I finished my last tour of duty, and my husband is from around here. So we retired back to this "green and pleasant land" before he…"

"I see. What's it like? All I hear are the stories from my grandma and her buddies. It's like they were expelled from Eden." He mimicked his grandma's wavering voice "Oh Simon, if I die before we are allowed home, will you scatter my ashes there?" He shook his head, dragging a hand through his Afro. "Even some of my friends talk about "reclaiming our homeland". Here there's a struggle with visas and such. What are the islands really like?"

"Well, Diego Garcia is now just a huge U.S. air-force and navy base. Your grandmother definitely would not recognize it. I took a couple of trips to the outlying islands. There is no one there now. It's just a big nature reserve. The few old buildings I saw had been reclaimed by the jungle. There is not even any animals, just lots of crabs. She was right about the weather though—it is hot all year round. The average temperature there would trigger a heat emergency in Crawley! The sea and the coral reefs are beautiful. And the birds are fantastic—frigate birds, brown noddies, shearwaters, red-footed boobies. I am a bit of a twitcher. A birdwatcher. It was a nice escape from the base."

"Why did you need to escape?"

"Well, being cooped up on an island smaller than Crawley, as a woman surrounded by thousands of American aircrew and sailors, had some challenges. The highest spot on the whole island is 9 metres above the high-water mark, so there was really nowhere to hide."

"Where did you live?"

"In barracks. I had a segregated unit. It was fairly basic, but at least there was aircon."

"And decent local food? The staple, judging by my grandma's get-togethers, is coconut fish curry."

"All the food we ate was imported. Standard American fare shipped in each month by container from Singapore. You can go off burgers pretty quickly."

"What a shame! It sounds boring."

"It was a busy time when I was there. I coincided with the Iraq War, so there were always B-52 bombers thundering along the runways and visits from all sorts of naval vessels. There were even some secret service types there for telecom and satellite work. You certainly feel very isolated. The nearest population of any size is 4 hours flight away, and that is only Mauritius."

"You ought to come along to one of the community lunches. There are usually some younger people there. The oldies like to speak creole, but it's mostly in English. They would be interested to hear your experiences. And the curry's not bad!"

"I don't think so. I wouldn't want to spoil their precious childhood memories. You'd need to be a wilderness survival expert to live there now. You know, there was no one living on the islands when the Spanish discovered them. So the "Chagossians" are the descendants of slave labour brought in by the French in the 18th century from Africa and South Asia to work the coconut plantations."

"We all have to come from somewhere, I suppose. Crawley was one of the first "New Town" established in 1946, as my Geography teacher was keen on telling us. And we already have an Olympic-sized swimming pool and can boast of Gareth Southgate as an old boy. Who knows what we could achieve on Chagos?! Perhaps we could change the name. Like New Caledonia or the New Hebrides, we could call it New Crawley! That sounds a lot less threatening. I really think you should come to the lunch. It would liven up the conversation. You never know, you might be able to go back there, on the boat when the islands are "liberated" and us Chagossians return home!" He gave an ironic clenched-fist salute.

"The UK government extended its lease of Diego Garcia to the U.S. till 2036, so don't hold your breath. We wouldn't want to anger our American allies. In return for the lease, I think they gave us a discount on some Polaris missiles."

"You should definitely come." He finished his Latte, tore off a corner of newspaper and wrote down for the lady the time and place of the next lunch. He made his way out through the delights of County Mall towards the bus stop. The old lady was still watching him as he stepped onto the escalator. He shouted "Long Live New Crawley!" which turned a few heads and made her laugh.

9

EXILE: RT

Bath. When the Duke of Connaught first said this word to me, I thought, my English not being so good, that he might be making a comment about my personal hygiene. Then I realised he was suggesting a place for me to stay. He said it would be quieter and more pleasant for my large family and entourage than residing in London. In retrospect, I realise he meant that it would be cheaper and also less embarrassing for the British government. At that time, they were leaning over backwards to appease Signor Mussolini in case, horror of horrors, he should ally with Herr Hitler. The British later even, shame on them, recognised "Italian East Africa", so temporarily extinguishing my country. Therefore, there was no official reception waiting for us at Waterloo station. No band or streamers. No meeting with King Edward or Prime Minister Balfour. I was just an embarrassment to be bundled off to the countryside. Ras Tafari, Haile Selassie, King of Kings, Lion of Judah in Bath. Absurd, but I lacked alternatives.

We were first sent to the Spa Hotel; we took over the whole west wing. I rather enjoyed the thermal baths. But the wealth that we had managed to carry with us was diminishing quickly. It was suggested to me, with no prospect of an early return to my homeland, that I might like to buy somewhere. I purchased Fairfield House, a villa big enough for us all on the edge of town, for £3,500. At one time, there was 25 of us living there. God, it was cold. The coal delivery was a time of rejoicing. Money grew tight. As I was no longer the legitimate government, there could be no official subsidies. But there were some small kindnesses. Sir Antony Eden arranged for carpets, curtains and cutlery to be transported from the palace in Addis, shipped free by P&O. There were some "anonymous donations". I also learnt later that the local council were covering our water and electricity bills. On a dreary day in January, two hundred locals each kindly paid 2s6d to attend an "At Home" to Fairfield for afternoon tea.

I write. I read. Fairfield has become an unofficial embassy. We receive refugees and news of my sad country. I hear of massacres and of family and friends killed or imprisoned. It has been frustrating to be stuck here, helpless. Sylvia Pankhurst has proved a true friend, publishing regular pamphlets on the situation in Ethiopia. I travel around and make speeches, repeating myself, warning of the dangers of appeasement: "It is us today, it will be you tomorrow." Locally, I am treated as a celebrity. I have already opened the Bath Horse Show and the Bath Dog Show. I have been given a tour of the only factory here, which makes Bath Oliver biscuits. Crowds of *faranjis* come to gawk. So I try to keep myself presentable: suits from Grieve & Hawkes, shoes from John Lobb, and my trademark cape well brushed.

After the weather, the hardest thing to get used to, and the main source of complaints from my family, is the impossibility of getting proper food. There is nowhere in Bath to buy injera bread or berbere spice. We just have to get used to the local food; there is one dish called "Sheperd's Pie" which is not bad. In my role as head of the orthodox church, I have also had to show ingenuity. The greenhouse has been whitewashed, and with the addition of a consecrated stone from Jerusalem, is now Bath's only chapel with services given in Amharic.

It was at the onset of the second winter that my wife decided to return to Jerusalem. The children, meanwhile, are busy being turned into little Englishmen and women, at public schools in Great Malvern, Taunton and Penzance. My eldest daughter plays her part, working as a nurse at St. Ormond Street hospital. The house has therefore grown slightly less full. For exercise each day, I take my dog, Rosa, for a walk around Royal Victoria Park. When, on our retreat from Ethiopia, HMS Enterprise picked up my party at Djibouti, the captain refused to board my two lions. Rosa was, however, allowed.

I believe our luck has now changed. Since Italy entered the war in June, the British government's attitude towards me is much improved. I have been told to prepare to depart to join General Wingate in Sudan. My son can go with me. Will I be sad to depart Bath? No. But I will retain a soft spot for those locals who treated me kindly. Perhaps someday, once this descendant of King Solomon and the Queen of Sheba, Father of the Nation, is safely re-established on his throne, I will revisit. And enjoy a spa.

10

Hamey "the Stranger"

Written on this 26th day of June, in the year of our lord 1597

To my beloved Sarah,

I write in the late evening but do not need a candle. So far North, and so close to the summer solstice, it barely turns dark. A friend at the Muscovy Company has told me he leaves on the morrow to take goods to Archangel for the summer sailing; he has promised to carry this letter. I have already managed to blot my script—please forgive me. It is not just my haste but also my excitement at the proposal I wish to make, as you will see.

It is your smile which has sustained me though my grim stay in this palace which has become a prison. I remember how excited I was on my way out—a young doctor, just graduated from Leiden, travelling to be "personal physician to the Tsar" on the recommendation of his professor. The romance of it! It was at Amsterdam port that I first saw your dear face. But I had little time for you, so eager was I in my pursuit of destiny, to make a name in this world. My long cold voyage through the White Sea dragged on my eagerness to start my duties. I ignored the signs I should have noted on my tedious journey inland through a drought-stricken countryside, impoverished by old wars. And so I arrived at the Kremlin.

Feodor Ivanovich was far removed from my expectation of what a Tsar should be. That is not to say he has been a bad master.

In fact I have come to feel rather sorry for him. Any son whose father has the nickname *grozny* or "inspires terror" is deserving of our sympathy. His father beat his elder brother to death in a fit of rage. His mother died when he was three. He lost his beloved wife Irina Godunova and their daughter did not survive childhood. So it is little wonder that he now spends most of his time at prayer. The actual running of the government lies in the hands of his brother-in-law, Boris Godunova, one-time *oprichnik*, that is to say, member of Ivan's personal guard. In my attendance on Feodor I see flashes of intelligence, however, it behoves him to play the "holy fool", for his own survival.

My professional duties are hardly demanding. My studies at Leiden, and my own work on anatomy, have led me to question some of the verities of Hippocrates and Galen, but Feodor suffers from a classic imbalance of the humours. I battle his excess of phlegm, brought on by Moscow's damp and cold, mostly through prescribing steam baths. In the time he can spare from prayer and bell-ringing, I have him bent over a steaming bowl of pepper-laden water, a cloth draped over his head. I have managed to introduce more vegetables, so scarce in winter, into his meat-heavy diet, but struggle to reduce his consumption of alcohol. Why they call it *aqua vitae* I cannot imagine—*aqua morta* would be more appropriate. Occasionally I need to purge his black bile with a theriac compound, but that is about the extent of my treatment. Otherwise I amuse myself with dissection—Moscow's winter is a fine preserver of dead bodies—and, in summer, botany—a chance to escape the foetid brick walls of the Kremlin with the excuse of the collection of herbs. I have written up the results of some of my work. I would be grateful if you could pass the papers in which this letter is wrapped to Johannes Heurnius with my warmest regards.

There are few people here with whom I can talk. The few

foreign ambassadors look down on me as some sort of tradesman unless, that is, a member of their family is sick, when they suddenly become polite. I occasionally take food with traders at the Muscovy company, but they mostly want to discuss broad cloth, beaver backs or cordage. There was an English doctor, Ridley, sent by Elizabeth in the hope of renewing trading privileges. But instead of the anticipated learned conversation and co-operation, he viewed me as a rival and constantly sought to contradict my recommendations. He did not last long. As for the local nobles, of course I was hampered by language. But it was not so much the ignorance that depressed me—they were generally knowledgeable about war, hunting and agriculture—but their total lack of curiosity outside these narrow bounds.

After three years, my loneliness mounts and my patience is exhausted. However, my application to leave has been rejected. Boris wants to attract foreign professionals to Moscow, to link this remote and parochial capital to the wider world from which it is cut off by Poles, Tartars and Livonians. So I have come up with a solution. The need for secrecy is what has made me write this letter in Dutch and wrap it in screeds of Latin medical theses. My excitement and what it promises has led to the blots.

My plan is to tell the Tsar that I am to marry you and that you will be arriving at Archangel on the Muscovy company's Spring sailing. I will, naturally, be travelling to meet you, to convey you and your trousseau back to Moscow. In fact you will <u>not</u> take the vessel. I will come to the port, leaving all my belonging in Moscow to allay any possible suspicion, then take the vessel back to Amsterdam, where we can be married, bringing only my savings. I realize that my proposal is forward, but, from your letters to me, I pray that it is not unwelcome?

I have long given up any hope of returning to my hometown of Bruges. Even Amsterdam, I believe, is not safe from the Imperial armies. I propose therefore that we find refuge in London. I have investigated the situation with friends at the Muscovy company. It is hard for a foreigner to get a license to practise in London, but this does not apply if you work privately for a patron. My contact is well connected to the Earl of Essex, and claims that we can find a place with this noble family and nearby accommodation. I have been able to accumulate quite a pot of cash here—I have not had to touch my annual salary of 1400 roubles as board and lodging is provided gratis and, frankly, there is little else on which to spend my money. I understand that it is a big step to take, for you to leave your family and travel overseas. But I am told that there is a large Flemish community in London, so we should not feel too out-of-place. Here I am called "Hamey the Stranger". I doubt I can be any stranger married and living in England.

You will not read this letter for at least three months. There will be no time for a reply to reach me. So I will act on my convictions and, trusting in Providence, hope to see your smiling face on the quay in Amsterdam.

In anticipation, your obedient servant

Hamaeus

11

Exile: O'Higgins

A bust overlooks the Thames by Richmond Bridge. A handsome soldier; epaulettes, long sideburns, and a thousand-yard stare. Cast into the darkened bronze is the suitably martial exhortation "VIVIR CON HONOR O MORIR CON GLORIA".

Below on the granite pedestal it explains:

GENERAL BERNARDO O'HIGGINS
1778-1842
CHILEAN STATEMAN
LIBERATOR OF HIS COUNTRY
LIVED AND STUDIED IN RICHMOND-UPON-THAMES
1795-1798

It is late September, so the wreath of flowers, laid at the foot of the monument by the Chilean ambassador on Independence Day, are only slightly wilted.

"For the Most Excellent the Marquess Osorno Don Ambrosio O'Higgins,

Viceroy of Peru, Lima

Richmond-upon-Thames

28th February 1799

My dearest father and benefactor, I pray Your Excellency will excuse my using this term so freely, for I do not rightly know whether

I may address you thus or not; but if I must choose between the two expressions, I will follow the inclinations of my nature (having no other guide), for had I different instructions I would obey them. Although I have written to your Excellency on several occasions, fortune has never favoured me with any reply, being seemingly hostile to me in this; but I trust that she will at length relent and grant my desires. Your Excellency must not think that I presume to complain, for in the first place this would be taking a liberty to which I have no right. I know it is to Your Excellency that I owe what education I have so far received. I am now twenty-one years old, and have not yet embarked on any career, not do I see any likelihood of doing so. I wish to join some naval academy if I can manage it, to learn the career to which I feel myself most attracted, and so hope that, as I have already written in previous letters which I trust Your Excellency received, you will decide about it as seems fit and proper, seeing that I feel myself well suited to it, and that a career of arms can bring advancement and honour with it at present, which is certainly what I would like and feel I have some aptitude for, so that I eagerly await Your Excellency's orders to obey and undertake as you dispose, confident that my duty and intention is only to please you. I will give your Excellency a brief account of the moderate progress which I am making here in my studies which are English, French, geography, history ancient and modern etc., music, drawing and the exercise of arms, in the last two of which I can say without boasting that I am tolerably proficient, and I should very much like to send Your Excellency some of my paintings, specially the miniatures, do not circumstances prevent it.

The Eeles family continues to treat me well. Their daughter Charlotte has become a particular friend. I fear, however, that I am become a burden on them, as the funds which were previously forwarded no longer arrive; I am concerned that the watchmakers in London through which the transfer was arranged may not be completely honest. I am sorry to mention such matters, but the winter here is especially damp and cold and I am in need of an overcoat. I am sorry to raise such petty matters with Your Excellency, who must be occupied with weighty matters of state and, I know, works hard for the best interests of so many thousands of Spain's subjects in the Americas. Just writing this word makes me long for home and family. I live in hope that we will one day meet and that you will believe me worthy of bearing your name.

Bernardo Riquelme."

"For Madame Charlotte Eeles,
Clarence House
Richmond-upon-Thames
England
18th September 1833

Dear Charlotte,

I can imagine your surprise when you receive this letter. Over the years I have often thought of your kindness to me when I was a homesick and, frankly, rather poor student in Richmond. I heard that an acquaintance of mine is due to travel to London and so, belatedly, have been spurred to write. It will be something of a miracle if these scribblings find you, but I have seen some miraculous events happen in my life, so God willing, they may find a way. It should be said that I am once more in exile, so have plenty of time, if no talent, for letter-writing.

I do not know whether you have followed the adventures of your erstwhile student? There is a vast ocean and high mountains between Richmond and Chile, so I suppose for you I have disappeared from the map. When I lived in your father's house, I doubtless confided in you about my father and my "irregular birth" to my blessed mother, unmarried and forty years my father's junior. You can imagine that boys, and indeed men, have used uglier words to describe my parentage. In the end I never did meet my father. He died before I could return, but on his death-bed he recognized me. His secretary told me that just four hours before his death he changed his will to leave me an estate with 3000 cattle in the South of Chile. The estate is long gone, but since that time I have used his name, as you can see by the signature below, rather than the surname of my blessed mother, by which you knew me. The remainder of my inheritance is the result of my Irish ancestors, namely my blue eyes, stocky build and a complexion that quickly colours under the sun. My father's secretary confided that, amongst his staff, he was known as "El Camaron" – the shrimp.

I now live at an estate called Montalvan, forty leagues South of Lima in Peru. By great good fortune my aged mother lives with me here. It is perhaps indelicate to ask, but have your own parents survived into old age? If so, please convey my best regards. There is also here my half-sister Rosita, two orphaned Araucanian girls, who are the delight of my old age, and my "natural" son Pedro. He was born on campaign, and his mother shifted her affections as my fortunes waned. It is a quiet life, but not without its small enjoyments. We grow sugar, and I work hard to improve our efficiency through mechanization. I am currently investigating the possibility of importing camels, which I think would do well here. I enjoy riding. I have a pet parakeet. I never touch alcohol, but am known to enjoy a pipe of tobacco.

Due to some wit, I suspect my estate manager, the outbuildings on the estate are named after my victories – El Roble, Chacabuco, Maipo etc. It is at El Roble that I am meant to have issued my now famous rallying cry "Live with honour or die with glory!" If I close my eyes, I can smell the cordite and hear the deafening noise of battle. Perhaps half-a-dozen men heard me and history has kindly simplified what I said and – forgive my insensitivity – deleted an expletive. There is no need to commemorate my numerous defeats. These are etched on my body. The most painful memento is the bullet hole in my shoulder. When the rains come and it aches, I curse the name of the Carrera brothers. I know that the Holy Church teaches us that we should forgive our enemies, but I cannot supress a deep satisfaction knowing that they are now just so much mouldering ash in a foreign field. The truth be told, I was never suited to politics. I am more at home on the battlefield, where I know where the enemy is and which way to charge. Too many men that I trusted have let me down. Still, I had my brief moment of glory as "Supreme Director" of an independent Chile. They called me "Father of the Nation". Not that I set any importance in titles; one of the acts of which I am most proud during my time in power is the abolition of aristocratic titles; adored equality is my idol. You can see, I was paying some attention when you were teaching me about the French revolution.

Whatever wrongs I may have done were the result of the difficult conditions in which it was my lot to govern. Trade and people's livelihoods had been damaged by the long war. Even nature seemed to revolt; I was in Valparaiso at the time of the earthquake and barely escaped with my life. It was the Junta that forced me out, not the people. On the way to the port, I still heard cries of "Viva O'Higgins!". We sailed out of Valparaiso on a British frigate and that was the last time I saw my homeland. Since leaving I have, of course, followed the chaos and anarchy that has descended upon my poor Chile. I have been approached by cabals to lead an invasion or coup, but I have no intention or wish to return.

Travelling the length and breadth of this land I have witnessed the physical proof of my father's achievement, albeit for the Spanish king; the cities founded, the roads built, the Indian tribes pacified, the international trade opened. I find that I, in contrast, have sacrificed my youth, health and fortune to mere fancies such as liberty and equality. It is for my father, a poor boy from County Sligo who rose to be Spain's Viceroy, that statues will be erected. I will sit here quietly, farming my land, feeding my parakeets and enjoying that family which is left to me.

I think fondly of our time together and hope that your memories do not differ too greatly from mine.

In gratitude,
Bernardo O'Higgins"

12

Exile: Eugenie

Camden Place

March 1873

Dr. Thomas W. Evans

Sir,

Should some historian uncover this letter, he may wonder why a French empress is writing to an American dentist. But, as we both know, I am now less than an empress, and you have always been a lot more than a dentist. You are a dear family friend who has stood by me throughout my tribulations. In those dark days of September 1871, had it not been for your help, I doubt I would have escaped the mob and been able to get across the Channel.

Camden Place is a long way from the Tuileries and Biarritz. The house is… *triste,* like a large and decaying café. Who could have foreseen that an Empress of France should end up in Chislehurst, Kent? The bathos! Please do not think me ungrateful for your arrangements. British aristocrats have offered us finer residences, but we did not wish to feel beholden. My diamonds and pearls fetched £60,000, which will support us for a while.

Queen Victoria has been kind. She visited Louis and myself when we were still … *en situation*. She is the godmother to my son,

Lou-Lou, the future Napoleon IV. I think she has eyes on my son for her daughter Beatrice. She has frequently invited me down to Osbourne. But England is so dull, so *démodé*. And the food! It is March, but I still have to light a fire in each room every day.

Do you realize we have now known each other over twenty years? I must have seemed such an ingenue, when I turned up that day with my mother, freshly arrived in Paris. Of course, you were already Louis' "Surgeon Dentist", and famous for your—*qu'est-ce que c'est*—"amalgum", so you were the first recommendation of our few Parisian acquaintances. You were so correct; I was always "the Countess of Teba". I think it must have taken ten years to persuade you to call me Eugenie. You were there on my wedding day and also the day after when I came to you with a raging toothache, which had not helped my wedding night!

Do you remember, the people called me "That Spanish Woman," just as they had called Marie Antoinette "that Austrian woman". The Bonapartes are only two generations from Corsican bandit, but it seems the *arriviste* must try harder. He needed an empress, and I was the prettiest girl to dare to resist his charms. My bedroom door remained firmly closed until the wedding night. Once I was pregnant, he quickly returned to his mistresses and whores. Oh, please do not misunderstand. That was fine with me. I would have just preferred a little more ... *discretion*. After one miscarriage, I produced a son and heir, my Lou-Lou, the Prince Imperial. That was it. *Fini*. I decorated my husband's arm at social events, charmed his friends and enemies, and slept alone.

You, who attended Louis for so long, are well aware of both his charm and his hypochondria. His "delicate teeth". He was already unwell before the war with Prussia. What a...*catastrophe*. I had expected Louis to find a glorious death on the battlefield of

Sedan. He looked so sad when he arrived at Dover, released from Prussian captivity. He had grown stout. His moustaches were no longer waxed and his goatee had turned grey. He did not long survive exile. The Napoleonic legend was not burnished by him dying of gallstones in Kent. So now I have laid him to rest in the local Catholic Church St. Mary's. This is hardly a suitable resting place for an emperor who did so much for his people. One day his body will be borne back to France and his many good deeds and achievements remembered.

I still have my Lou-Lou – such a handsome boy. He graduated top of his class from the academy in fencing and riding. He insists on establishing his military credentials, so, thanks to his doting godmother Victoria, he is now in South Africa with the British Army fighting some heathens called "Zulu". The Queen promised her staff will keep him well away from the action. The irony – a Bonaparte fighting for the English.

You are most welcome to visit; it would be lovely to see you again and be reminded of better times. I know it is difficult, but I would be most grateful if you could bring any of my belongings – perhaps some small items from the collection at Fontainebleau? I refuse to play the part of the fading little widow, pining away in sad exile. When this new *République* falters, our time will come again. Meanwhile, there are connections to make and a world to see.

Yours very sincerely,
Eugenie

13

Exile: BaA

January 22nd 1994

Dear Asma,

It is early. My taxi to Heathrow is booked. I am sorry to leave without saying goodbye in person, but I received bad news last night. My brother was killed in a car accident. My handsome, talented elder brother managed to wrap his red Ferrari around a pylon on the road to Damascus airport. So I have been summoned back to attend his funeral with a one-way ticket.

I hope that we can meet again, but I fear it will not be in London. I enjoyed my time here. I suffered from the cold and wet, of course, but I at least I had my nice, warm flat, just around the corner from work, convenient for Baker Street tube. I have packed what I can, but in all the rush, I am sure I will have forgotten something. If so, could you post it to me? I have left the key in the normal place. There is still three months to run on the lease. I could get the embassy staff to help, of course, but there is some personal stuff, so I would appreciate your help.

I will send a separate letter of resignation to the hospital. I will miss my colleagues in the Western Eye's ophthalmology department. Occasionally I would overhear the nurses making fun of me—"the giraffe"—or copying my lisp. But it was only banter, and we got on well enough. I will even miss the patients. I was finally able to make some use of all those years of training to actually help people. I think I was quite good at it. For most of them I was doubtless just another foreign NHS doctor, gawkily tall with a small moustache. But they were clearly grateful for my help.

I really thought I'd escaped. My dashing elder brother would take over the family business. My father let his geeky second-son go abroad to further his medical studies; what parents don't want a doctor in the family? Now my pass has been cancelled. In retrospect, I should have made more of my time here, not that a junior doctor has many free hours. Perhaps playing PC games and listening to a Walkman was not the best use of my time. We should have gone to more concerts. That Phil Collins one last month was brilliant. But you know I had to keep a low profile. You saw what happened when I met other Syrian expats; it was embarrassing. They'd either clam up, or start fawning over me. That why it was so nice to be able to visit your parents' house, old friends of my family. I could be myself and enjoy some proper Syrian home cooking. Your father being a doctor himself also helped.

Now I need to wade back into a battleground of tribes and religions, Shi'ites and Sunnis, Alawis, Druze and Isma'ili's, Jews and Christians. Instead of plastic coffee from the machine on the 2nd floor and a tuna sandwich from the deli, there will be champagne and canapes. Instead of pensioners worried about cataracts in the antiseptic corridors of the Western, there will be ministers and ambassadors in marble mansions, all with their hands out.

Syria is the al-Assad family business, and has been since Father eliminated the last of his rivals in 1970. But you know me well enough to see that I am entirely unsuited to run it. I have, on occasion, fondly imagined that I could make a contribution to Syria's healthcare and education, something I know about. But how am I going to make any progress against that *shilla* of old generals, fossilized bureaucrats and relatives with their hands in the till. Our name might now be al-Assad, "the Lion", but only because my grandfather changed it from al-Wahsh, "the Savage". Perhaps I can persuade Father that someone else should take this poisoned chalice. My younger brothers, as much as a love them, are even less suited than me. My sister Bushra and husband could do it, but Syria has not been ruled by a woman since Queen Zenobia, and she commanded the world's best armoured cavalry. Perhaps there is an uncle who could do it? Not Rifaat, of course, after what happened when Father had that heart attack in 1984. Frankly, I am surprised Rifaat still breathes.

The problem for whoever else who takes over is that the mere existence of an elder son abroad, however innocuous, would be a sword over their heads. Unbearable. I would never be safe. So, as much as I want to, I cannot say "No". Perhaps the best is that I try, fail, then get sent into exile—preferably somewhere warmer than London, with a decent music scene and an appreciation of proper eyecare.

I can see through the curtains that my taxi is waiting downstairs in the pouring rain, so I better go. I will post this from the airport with my last 1st class stamp. I appreciate your help. When the funeral is over and I have had a chance to see the lay of the land, perhaps you can visit? I know you need to complete your studies at King's, but it would be nice to see a friendly face amongst the jackals. Perhaps you can become President of the Syrian Computer society!

Your friend,

"Doctor" Bashar

14

The Wrong Place

Drinks this time were to be held at the Queen's Head pub. The monthly college get-together normally takes place at the Volunteer pub—the one just off Pall Mall—but this time they'd booked a place up past Oxford Circus. Perhaps, because it was Christmas drinks, they were expecting a better turnout? The normal meet-up barely filled one table. None of the regular attendees were from his own year group, but Ben's apartment was nearby and the drink was subsidized. Also, with his youngest still taking her A levels, he felt that it might be smart to keep in touch with his old college. Just in case…

The invite had said 6.30pm to 8. He was always early at events, especially when it was at a new location. He was a man who liked to know where he was going, and get there in good time. So, he found himself slouching past the Queen's Head—he had the right address—at an unfeasibly early 5pm. Perhaps he should get something to eat first? Something to line his stomach before the drinking. He found a tapas place nearby. He never went anywhere without reading matter, so he was able to while away the intervening time, sipping on a glass of rather rough house red, and eating a couple of inexpertly chosen dishes.

It was 6.20, so time to make a move. He tapped his credit card on the machine to pay his bill—service had been included at a generous 12.5% he noticed—then went back out into the damp cold of a December evening in London. The man who normally organized these college events was a short, stout, bald chap with thick-lensed glasses. Ben did not know his name. Now that they had met so often, it was too embarrassing to ask. Sure enough, as he pushed open the door of the Queen's Head, there was the short, stout, bald chap already at the bar. Ben greeted him warmly and the host asked "Would you like a drink?"

"A pint of Bitter, please". He actually would have preferred a G&T, but because he came from Yorkshire, he felt that drinking Bitter was more on-brand. "How come you chose this place, rather than the pub we normally go to?" The short, stout, bald chap looked slightly puzzled, but then said "There were some thefts at the other place. You know, pick-pockets." He handed over the foam-topped beer.

"Thanks. Oh, that's a shame. But this place seems nice. Cozy." He was not sure where to take the conversation next. He remembered that the stout, short, bald chap worked in the Civil Service, at the Department of Statistics, so that was a no-go area. "Have many of the group arrived yet?"

"They are just round here." The organizer led him to a corner table, weaving through a noisy post-work drinks crowd. There were six people around the table. He joined them, sitting opposite the host. He did not recognize the others, but that was not unusual; he had matriculated over 40 years ago. The topic of conversation, however, was a typical one—they were talking about their children's achievements. A daughter enjoying her first term at Cambridge. A son taking a gap year in Asia before heading to film school. He kept quiet, occasionally sipping his beer whilst listening for an opening in the conversation. The handsome man next to him—silver-grey hair swept behind his ears, designer stubble, cashmere jumper—was asked from across the table "So what are you working on now?" "The second series of "The Last Casualty". We have had a few casting issues, but it's going OK." It seemed from the follow-up questions that the man worked in TV production. This was unusual. Ben's college produced a lot of lawyers, some PR/marketing types and a few teachers, but this was the first alumni he'd met who had gone into entertainment.

After a while the handsome man, looking to include him in the conversation, asked: "So, where do you know this reprobate from?" gesturing at the organizer. "Oh well, I know him from Oxford. We've met at a few college events before."

"You never told me you went to Oxford, you sly devil." Mr. Handsome smirked at Mr. Stout, who laughed at the idea: "Not me. I went to the University of Life."

Mr Handsome turned to Ben: "You really had me going then! You said it with such a straight face. I see I am going to have to watch you." He turned back to the others, who were taking it in turn to discuss the projects they were involved in. He was sitting at a whole table-full of TV producers. This wasn't right. The realization gradually dawned that he was sitting with entirely the wrong group of people. This wasn't the college Christmas get-together. He was not sure how to extract himself. He had drunk one-quarter of what now appeared to be a free pint, extorted under false pretences.

Eventually, shame-facedly, he leaned towards Mr. Stout and said quietly: "I seem to have made a mistake. I came here for a college get-together and thought I recognized you. I'd better go and find my own group." He gestured at his now half-drunk pint: "Can I buy you a drink?"

"No. Don't worry about it. That's all right."

"Sorry about that". Grasping his pint, he nodded farewell to the TV producers and slunk towards the bar. Sure enough, there was an upstairs private room booked for the college. As he put his foot on the stairs he heard a howl of laughter from the TV producers' table.

In the room upstairs, he recognized a couple of the college regulars. The sideboard was lined with bottles of Chilean wine. "Oh, you didn't have to buy your own drink" said a lady near the door who he nearly recognized. "But well done. More for the rest of us!"

Here the talk was mostly of the latest political scandals. Travel plans for the Xmas holidays. He discussed the state of education for a while with an Indian gentleman who taught engineering at a school he might know—Westminster? One woman had come down all the way from Kendal for the event. The conversation downstairs had been more interesting. He rather regretted that he had not brazened it out. He made his excuses and slipped out early. Perhaps it was still possible to catch the second half of his team's mid-week football match on TV.

15

Exile: Ovidius

Zlobv qeb xqqxzfba ql qeb Mxixqkfb. Al vlro ybpq ql fkqolzrba fq ql qeb zfobiz jlofz lro xdxfkd Glsb. F jlkv qexq vlr exsb ybqqbo zlkkaqbkflk jfqe qeb Dloldk, yrj tb xbk bsboq ifiib eboi lk lbo rjyoxbflrp plk. F exsb ixfa fq ql qefziv qfjb, yrj xii jlbo prqyib zljjkfzqqfkflk exsb ybbk fk sxfk. Alk'q tloov xyrlq qeb zlkqbkpq. Vlr jlkv ylkr vlro erpyxrya obzloa qexq F tfii yb fk qeb yxzh olv lc xk xojv.

Afpqoryfqb qeb lqebo bofkqibp xp plervk. F txp yrpv ivpq tfkqbo. Qebp bibidvp dl ql xkv cofkbka xka xzxfdrxexzbfbp, ylqe ivxixa xka afplvxiva, jelk jfdeq exsb qeb box lc qeb dobxq. Qexq cxq pirx Zlqqx pbkq jb x mobpbkq lc x pfisbo moloxqfq lc qeb Fjmboifx cxfjfiv. F exsb erkd fk fk qeb ixqofkb clo obdrsxio xka molkcerka zlkpfdefqfkflk. Fk obkqro F pbkq efj x nfscbo lc Pzvqefx xooltp. F clzzbpba qefq fkjb lk qeb zfobiz xoxolk Dbojxdfzrp. Fc vlr pbb Jxufjrp, qbii efj F exsb hbqo zlmvbp lc xii qefq, pl qebbo tfii yb xklqebo yllh ql mryfpej qbbo qeb zlxpq fp zibxo—tloifkd qfibp "Pxa Plkdp"—ibpp jxobqbxibp qexk "Qeb Xoq lc Axiifxizb", F xafjq, yrj F xj pxa. Qbii efj F exsb molfpeba "Jbqxjloelmbp" xka "Cxpqf". F xj abkqfojfkb ql yb obxa.

Qeb cofopq zxmqfxfk fkqo mlkq, jbbo qeb fzb jbiqbka, obixvb qeb orjlrk qexq lro Glsb jxv pllk yb qbpqfkd fij lk fjkloqfiv. Tfqe xrdrsqrp dlkb, qebbo fp ifiib obxplk clo vlr ql objxfk fk Oljb. Fq exp ybbk clo yboq fpfb qbo xka bboevlkb pffc jfqe jv zljifxqbp.

Vlro axexqebo fp klv pxciv jxofba xka jlsba ql Klqeo Cxfbzx jfqe, xp Zlqqx abpzofyba efj, "qeb abmfixqba lpqofzbe". Pbii lro zlkqrovo molobqv xka zljb eboi; fk lro zxpb Mboebklib tfii cfka efj Laxfppbrp. Pxif qefp prjjbo. Al klq txfq rkfiv vbxo-bka; jv elzoba Tfkqbo sflxdb pfiif cfiip jv fkfdeqobpq jfqe pefjsbobzp. Yofkd xp jrzbe lc jv objxfkfkd ifyxoxiv xp vlr zxk. Bpbfzifxv Zfzboh; elv afa eb bpxmb afif fk grpq lkb vbxo? Qeb ilkd tfkqbo xpfab, Qljfp fp klq xxa xp F molqoxv. Qebbo xop exozap xka sflaxxkap fkifxka. Xmxoq ylkr txljfkd jv yba, F kbba vlro eboi jfqe qeb elprbexla. Qeb clla fp qboofyib. F xipv kbba x ifsb xrdfkbzb clo jv moljbp; tofqfkd x moljb jfzbe zxkklq yb obxa fp ifhb axkzfkd fk qeb axoh. F txp bbsbk asfskb ql tofqb x moljb fk qeb ilzixa mxqlfp; jv pexddv xrdfkbzb peltba qebfo xmmobzfxqfkflk.

Fc F xj mxokabka, tb zxk obqrok ql Oljb fk qorfjre. Fc klq, vlr zxk qxhb yxz zbp. F al klq txkq jv ilkibv dlpq ql txkaba lk qeb Yixzh Pbx'p pfkpfqbo zlxpq.

F jlkv bknzobqfkflk fp tbxoifpjb, yrj tb exsb fbxokq qeb zlpq lc rktxov yixqebo. Dfskb jv bozqfz molbqv xka (rkboxkba) obmrxqxfkflk, qefp kbtiv jloxi obdfjb, qeb evmzlzqfqbp, txp grpq txfqfkd clo xk bzrpb ql yb afa lc jb. Jv pqrfaf qloxzixkzb clo qelpbo cliipt xkxkfkd x obqrok ql x obmryfz txp bksre.

Clo qeb kbsq fbbqbo, pefq qeb bknzobqfkflk hbv xp xddobba. Yrok qefp klqb.

"O glory, O image of the country that flourishes through you,
O hero to match the very sphere you rule –
So may you dwell on earth, yearned for by heaven,
So may you pass late to your promised stars!
Spare me, I beg you: just cancel a minor portion of your grudge against me.
What remains will be punishment enough for my inept frivolity.

Two offences undid me – a poem and an error. But your anger is moderate.
You spared my life, I've kept my civic rights and status: my fortune has not been assigned to others,
Nor, by the terms of your edict, am I pronounced an "exile" – all things I feared, since I deserved them.
You ordered me "relegated" via Scythian waters to a long view of the Pontic steppe.
It's not so much the eternal cold that crucifies me,
Or because the barbarian's language is alien to Latin,
As that here I'm in a hard-pressed enclave, see fighting at close quarters,
With only a low wall that barely holds the enemy at bay.
When the Danube is frozen level by the ice-dry wind-chill
Hordes of hostile savages ride over on swift ponies, their pride,
And cut a marauding swath through the countryside.
Poor peasants flee. Their property, unguarded, makes quick loot.
Others die, those sharp barbed arrows through them,
Die in agony, for the flying steel is smeared with venom.
Look, I'm not against suffering, I'd just like to suffer more safely. Would you mind?
Ovid is gone. What pleasure do you get from stabbing this dead body?
There is no space in me now for another wound."

Convey this to the Palatine. Do your best to introduce it to the circle which orbits our ageing Jove. I know that you have better connections with the Gorgon, but we can expect little help from her or her umbrageous son. I have laid it on thickly this time, but more subtle communications have so far all been in vain. Don't worry yourself about the part about the fighting. You know from your husband's military record that I will be in the back row of any army.

Distribute the other epistles as shown. As you see, I have been busy writing all last, long winter. These elegies go to friends and acquaintances, both loyal and disloyal, who might have the ear of the great. That fat slug Cotta sent me a present of a silver portrait of the Imperial family. I have hung in in the latrine for regular and profound consideration. In return I send him a quiver of Scythian arrows. I focus this time on the circle around Germanicus. If you see Maximus, tell him I have kept copies of all this work, so there will be another book to publish once the coast is clear – working title "Sad Songs" – less marketable than "The Art of Love", I admit, but I am sad. Tell him I have polished "Metamorphoses" and "Fasti". I am determined to continue to be read in Rome, even though I cannot go there myself.

The first captain into port, once the ice melted, relayed the rumour that our Jove may soon be testing his own immortality. With Augustus gone, there is little reason for you to remain in Rome. It has been four years since my relegation and everyone must be bored stiff with my complaints. Your daughter is now safely married and moved to North Africa with, as Cotta described him, "that depilated ostrich". Sell the country property and come here; in our case Penelope will find her Odysseus. Sail this summer. Do not wait until year-end; my own forced Winter voyage still fills my nightmares with shipwreck. Bring as much of my remaining library as you can. Especially Cicero, so I can work out how he escaped exile in just one year. The long winter aside, Tomis is not as bad as I portray. There are orchards and vineyards inland. Apart from warming my bed, I need your help with the household. The food is terrible and the staff truculent. I also need a live audience for my poems; writing a poem which cannot be read is like dancing in the dark. I was even driven to write a poem in the local patois; my shaggy audience seemed to appreciate it.

If I am pardoned, we will return to Rome in triumph. If not, you can carry back my ashes. I do not want my lonely ghost to wander here on the Black Sea's sinister coast.

I know encryption is wearisome, but we have learnt too well the cost of unwary blather. Given the erotic poetry written in my youth, the newly moral regime—the hypocrites—was just waiting for an excuse to be rid of me. My naive tolerance for those old fools wanting a return to a republic was enough.

For the next letter, shift the encryption key as agreed. Burn this note.

16

Exile: PP

"Not a bad pad for an exile, eh?" He gestured at the plush furnishings of the expensively rented Mayfair apartment. "Or perhaps you think this is my natural habitat? 'The Sultan of Berkeley Square'!" I had seen on television how he had flown in on his private Boeing 737 and then been ferried to this address in a chauffeured Jaguar with his beautiful (second) wife. The message was clear—I am still rich and have what it takes. One could easily start to resent this showing off, but then "But how are you, Elizabeth? You are looking well; I like the hairstyle, it suits you. It has been a long time." We both knew exactly how long—17 years. That was when he jumped bail and fled the country from a Dorset airfield on a light aeroplane. The truth is that we were both looking older. He had lost his Hollywood good looks—he is 69 after all—but still presents well. Pale grey suit and tie. Matching handkerchief in the top pocket.

I had been one of the last believers—even after the raid by the Serious Fraud squad, and through the long preparations for a trial which never happened. I had lost a lot in the company's collapse, but could afford to be more philosophical than some of my fellow investors, so had kept in contact. I suppose that was why I was being granted this audience.

"Well, it is nice to see you back in the country, Mr. Nadir."

"Asil, please."

"I must admit that I am surprised. You seemed well-settled in North Cyprus with your new businesses—the newspaper, the hotels. Your family and relatives are all there and the UK authorities could not extradite you. The weather is certainly better! But now here you are, back voluntarily to face trial. Can I ask why?"

"I was innocent in 1990 and I am innocent today. Yes, I could live out my life in Cyprus, but, after all I achieved, I don't want to go down in history as a fraud. I created employment and wealth for so many. I gave to charity. But all this will be forgotten if I cannot clear my name."

"The newspapers are pretty hostile. How confident are your lawyers?"

"They say that there is clear evidence of the SFO mishandling evidence, so they believe that the case will be dismissed."

"That's great news. What will you do once it's all resolved? Will you stay here?"

"Well, I am old now, but I think I still have time to make back something of what we lost. Of course, I have family in Cyprus, and obligations to the government—still hardly anybody recognizes them apart from Turkey, but they were supportive at a difficult time. However, North Cyprus is a very small stage. To think I bought a tiny East-end textile firm for just 5p per share in 1979 and by 1981 the shares reached £35. I turned it into a FTSE100 company. Those were the glory days."

"So, I have good news to tell the ladies. Can I say that there will be some…recompense?"

"I think that some repayment will be part of the settlement, but please ask them to moderate their expectations."

"If the case is just thrown out on technicalities, how will you address all the accusations that were made? About taking money from the company."

"You are quite right. My plan is the find some sympathetic journalists and investors..." he gestured towards me "to spread the word." He leaned forward and lowered his voice, as though he was going to impart some secret for my ears alone.

"The first thing we need to do is to explain the background, how it was in the market of the '80's. It is already over 20 years ago, and many have forgotten, if they ever knew. There were plenty of companies that grew rapidly through leveraged mergers and acquisitions. Perhaps Tiny Rowland's Lonrho will ring a bell? The Hanson Trust? After the "global financial crisis" we are now all so sober, focussing on our "core competencies". Then it was all go-go. We acquired the citrus plantations in Cyprus, a packaging line in Famagusta, the Del Monte Fruit brand, the Sansui Electric brand. Just like other conglomerates, we borrowed money to make these acquisitions. A rising share price made it easier to borrow more money, so I used company money to buy our own shares. There is nothing illegal about that. When the SFO raided our offices in 1990, spurred on by rumour and all those who envied my success, they were looking for signs of insider trading. They found none and dropped that charge. But it was already too late. So much in business is based on confidence, and it was shattered." He paused, reaching for a bottle in a cooler on the sideboard. "Would you like some champagne? It's 1996."

I would have accepted a glass of champagne whatever the vintage. As he reached over to fill my glass, the cuff of his shirt rose up. "I see you are still wearing that watch."

He smiled fondly. "I have nicer watches, but I thought I would wear this one for the trip to remind the powers-that-be of just how much I did for Margaret and the Tories." He slid the watch off his wrist to show me the inscription on the back: it read "Don't let the buggers get you down."

"A Minister for Northern Ireland lost his job over that, but I still have the watch."

"How will you handle the charges of taking money from the company?"

"Once they had given up on the insider trading, they needed a new charge. They simply do not understand the way we do business in the Eastern Mediterranean. We like to have plenty of cash on hand, so we can respond quickly to events. Also, our immediate families are trusted and involved in the business. For every pound that I took from the account in the UK, I deposited the equivalent in Turkish Lira in our bank in Cyprus. The same goes for loans to family members." He had raised his voiced. "It is all there in the accounts. It is not my fault if analysts focussed on the profit and loss account rather than the balance sheet."

"But the newspapers say that the complicated web of affiliates proves that you were trying to hide something."

"That is just to impress the ignorant. If the UK tax code allows legitimate methods to minimize tax—by routing business through Jersey or Switzerland—then of course I should use it. Shareholders should criticize me if I didn't! The journalists are also aware of our connections in Cyprus, and how the island's partition has given us economic opportunities in the North, but they just like to use these names to make us sound alien and exotic. Do you know not one member of the SFO ever visited Cyprus to confirm the situation on the ground?! <u>There</u> is the real scandal".

He slumped back as if exhausted. His suit trousers had ridden up in the excitement of his defence and I saw the security tag secured above an ankle. He saw me notice, and tugged down his trousers to cover it again. "Such a nuisance. Anyway, how is Alex? Do I have your husband's name correct?"

The Queen v. Asil Nadir took almost two years to get underway. On August 23rd 2012, in the Central Criminal Court, the Honourable Mr. Justice Holroyde made his sentencing remarks. He concluded that the accused was "a man of outstanding business skills and considerable charm" who had "brought employment and financial benefit to many persons around the world." He also admitted that the SFO had been untruthful on the legal issue raised by the defence, but felt that it had no effect on the fairness of the trial. The judge admonished the accused that the company's money was not his money and found him guilty of "theft on a grand scale."

Asil Nadir was convicted of 10 offences of theft from Polly Peck International totalling £29m. Taking into consideration mitigating circumstances, such as his voluntary return to stand trial, time under curfew and health, Asil Nadir was sentenced to 10 years in prison. In 2016, he was transferred to a prison in Turkey, where he spent one night, before being released and returning to North Cyprus.

17

A Local Dispute

Dear Sherry,

Bad news, I'm afraid. I know I must sound like a broken record, but the local lawyers assure me that, even by the standards of Malta's snail-like legal system, eight years is excessive. It's not like the case is complicated; it's just a contract dispute over some Valletta property. Of course, there was the Covid pandemic delay. And the Plaintiff's architect didn't bother to show up twice. But still...

I know, I know. I am as keen as you to get my hands on my share of the money held by the court. Yes, 164,000 Euro would pay quite a lot of bills. I understand.

Today was marked for my cross-examination. So I flew in last night from Shanghai. I'm jet-lagged to hell—these long-haul flights seem to get harder as I get older. The first flight to Istanbul was full, so I didn't get much sleep. Then I messed around in the Turkish Airlines lounge, drinking lentil soup, till the next flight started boarding. Maybe I shouldn't have had those extra glasses of red wine, but they were free. You always used to criticise me for passing up on bargains. To save money, I'm staying in an AirBnB in Sliema, so I had to struggle out of bed to catch the first ferry to Valetta. I was in a bad mood, but the sunshine and sea-air still lifted my spirits as we chugged towards the honey-coloured jumble of fortresses and towers. Do you remember when we first saw it together from the top deck? Twelve years ago now. I said "Perhaps we could live here" and you smiled. Decent food, wine weather and low tax. What's not to like? I sometimes wonder, if we really had moved here, would we still be together?

You were just accompanying me on a business trip, for me to see whether my company could make use of Malta's favourable tax laws—it's in the EU, sunnier than Dublin, cheaper than Luxembourg. But my question wasn't totally out of the blue. We'd had vague discussions about eventually leaving China, finding a better place to bring up our son. Now here was this intriguing place. Obviously further from your family, but closer to my remaining relatives in England. We could both be foreigners here together.

I remember you googling for Malta's best school back at the hotel that evening. You quickly concluded there wasn't one, but we already knew Paul was not going to be an academic superstar, so that wasn't a deal-breaker. Also, Valletta property prices seemed reasonable, though, in comparison to Shanghai, most places look cheap. I remember you asking why there was such a large amount of derelict property in the heart of the city. Now we know. But then we were young, naïve and already had one successful construction project under our belts. When the estate agent took us around, I caught the look in your eyes when we went up onto the roof and saw its panoramic view of the Grand Harbour. If we could build a living room with this view…

So "Operation Ruined Palazzo" began. You have criticized me for plenty of things, but I don't remember you raising particular objections at that time. Of course, with the benefit of hindsight, I should have done more research. I should have insisted on meeting the sellers, but they lived in Holland, so it was all handled through third parties. When I was told that the seller's architect was already working on building permission for a roof-top construction, it looked as though it would be fine, with suitable amendments. No need to start again. I took them on good faith—a gentleman's word is his bond and all that. That's why I agreed to pay the 164,000 Euro bonus if the sellers could obtain the amended building permission within one year. Talk about providing a hostage to fortune…

Perhaps, if I'd asked around, I'd have found out that the neighbour had objected to previous proposed plans. I might even have discovered that the neighbour happened to be a well-connected lawyer with the Malta Environment & Planning Agency. But Malta, as I soon learned, is a small, closed society, where it is difficult for outsiders to break in. I thought I was protected by our agreement. I wasn't to know that, under pressure from his clients to meet the one-year limit, the seller's architect would cave in and make any concessions necessary to gain permission, without letting my architects know. Our much-desired room-with-a-view turned into a long, thin corridor.

It is important to remember that I got all our capital back. When, after several years trying to get the right kind of permission, I decided to sell-out, we even made a small profit. Of course, all the back-and-forward travel, all the uncertainty, took its toll. But you got your share of the proceeds. Now I have just got to get back the money held by the court to cover this pending "bonus" claimed by the bloody sellers. I've still never met them. The court has now been earning interest on my money, our money, for eight long years. I guess we are helping fund Malta's budget deficit, whilst creating employment for the local legal profession.

So here we are. After getting an espresso boost, I made my way at the appointed time to my lawyer's office, red-eyed and twitchy. Like most of Valletta's lawyers, their chambers are, ironically, in Strait Street. We had a quick discussion on tactics. I put on my tie. This was my second time in court, so I had a better idea what to expect. The previous time the cross-examination was prorogued to allow checking of the original of a redacted photo-copy presented by the prosecution. This caused another two-month delay. At the scheduled time we went to the Law Courts. They are directly opposite St. John's Cathedral—remember, the one we visited on our trip? The OTT cathedral, decorated with plunder from centuries of piracy in the name of the Pope. After an airport-style bag check and pat-down, the lawyers put on their robes. No-one seemed to be occupying our allotted courtroom (all the doors have a little window so you can see what's happening inside) so we filed in.

The judge, in this case a lady, sat at the front of the small, dark-panelled courtroom on a raised dais. There was also an assistant, who conveyed documents from the lawyers to the judge, and a recorder. Both of these also were women. I was told to sit on one of the uncomfortable wooden seats that lined both sides. The lawyers gathered around a central table, like a murder of crows around some fresh carrion. The only decoration was a red and white Maltese flag and, on the wall above the judge, a gruesome, crucified Christ. On the dock, however, either side of the microphone, there was both a Bible and a Quran. Last time they also offered that I could swear a humanist oath, but, in a solidly Catholic country, I thought it would look better to swear on the Bible.

We were all ready to start, except the prosecutor had not arrived. My lawyer went out to try to find him. He was called "Borg" which is the most popular of Malta's limited list of surnames, so there was no point shouting his name down the corridor. He was on the way—ETA 20 minutes. To make best use of the court's time, it is was decided to start another hearing. I sat on one of the hard chairs, twiddling my thumbs and trying to look innocent. It's hard enough to understand what's going on in an English court, but here business is conducted in Maltese, a language three parts Arabic to one part Italian. Given the combination of difficult language and Legalese, I understood about as much as if I'd been at a meeting of Norwegian freemasons. I caught more when your family argued in Shanghai dialect over dinner.

Having a good chance to observe my fellow attendees, I realized that all the men in the court were bald. My own lawyer bears a strong resemblance to Mussolini. It appears to be an island-wide genetic legacy. So it's funny that the lawyers here don't wear wigs. Maybe it's just too hot?

Borg eventually turned up, looking sheepish. The judge's opening volley, in English, was "This man has just flown from Asia to be here, and you can't even make it across town in time?" Good to start with a small moral victory. From the way Borg was anxiously flipping through his files, you could see he barely knew which courtroom he was in.

I was called to the dock, feeling self-conscious, like a bad actor in one of those detective series we used to binge. After the oath, the judge asked whether I had the original document that was in question last time. I said I did and handed it over. The judge glanced at the document, then turned to the prosecutor and said: "Very well, please continue with your questions." Borg replied "I have no more questions." That was it. I'd just flown 6000 miles to hand over one sheet of paper that the judge already had on file. My own lawyer then lobbed a couple of soft questions so I could explain to the judge what was wrong with the seller's planning permission. Then "You are free to go". Outside, my lawyer told me that both sides now have 3 months in which to submit their summing ups and meet before the judge. My attendance is not required, thank God. I can expect a judgement "as soon as next year". Unless, that is, there is an appeal, which might add another 2 or 3 years. I know you don't trust me, but I'm really doing my best to get the money back.

I had mentally written off the whole morning for the case, so felt an idiot in my dark suit in the bright sunshine amongst all the tourists with a day to fill. I couldn't stop myself from walking over to look at our house. Someone else has already done it up. Must be someone with better local connections than me. Here I'll always be as much of a foreigner as I am a "laowai" in Shanghai.

Tomorrow I'll catch a flight over to gloomy England and the boarding school. It will doubtless be pissing it down in Sevenoaks. I'll let you know how Paul is after I've seen him. I know he's a good boy and calls his mother every week-end, when he's not busy swimming, sailing or off on school trips, that is. I'll also let you know what his house master says. He's usually complimentary, as long as I'm up-to-date on the school fees.

Yours,

The Foreigner

18

~~Redacted~~

From the desk of Charles Stewart, Head of Communications

Dear Jonathan,

I attach an edited version of your memo to the board. Please forgive my presumption—I know that the CFO role is new to you, and you must wonder why an internal company memorandum needs to be edited in such a way. The problem is that we used to be a public utility, so all documents must stand up to scrutiny by the regulator or any other party who might not have the best interests of our major shareholders at heart. I am not saying that there is anything here which Ofwat could object to, but it is best not to leave any hostages to fortune!

I appreciate your understanding.

Yours sincerely,

Charles

Attachment: Memorandum to board on proposed ~~re-~~financing

At a time when ~~Ofwat~~ the Water Services Regulation Authority is demanding increased spending to repair and maintain our water and sewage system, this memorandum outlines the ~~difficult~~ challenging state of company finances and possible solutions.

- Net debt at the company has now topped £8bn, or eight times shareholder equity. This ~~high~~ level of debt, combined with the trend of rising interest rates and the well-publicised ~~news~~ rumours of financial difficulties at Thames Water, means that our traditional sources of bank loans and bond finance are ~~effectively~~ temporarily closed to us.
- We have already disposed of all of the ~~gas, telecom and waste~~ non-core assets acquired in the U.K. and overseas in the 1990s boom. The property development division was, ~~fortunately~~, disposed of in a timely fashion just before the pandemic.
- The room for further cost-cutting measures seems limited. The workforce has already been halved and further cuts would seem to go against the call for improved service levels from the regulator. Cost saving efforts were offset by the £2.1m fine imposed last year for ~~sewage spills~~ environmental events.
- The regulator has shown that it will currently not approve any further mergers or acquisitions within the water sector in the U.K. so it appears that no further savings can be achieved through increasing scale. We should, however, redouble efforts, together with our peers, to persuade the government that water fees should be increased to help necessary upgrades to the old and badly-maintained system that was privatized by the Thatcher government in 1989. [Good! This should play well with the new government]. ~~By not allowing appropriate fees and then complaining about the service it seems as though the politicians are both having their cake and eating it.~~
- Our share price stands close to a multi-year low, so our broker advises that a new equity issue would not be welcomed at this time. Savings could be made on the

~~relatively generous~~ dividend we pay, but I have been told by visiting institutional investors that this provides the main support for our share price, so it is a matter which the board should consider carefully before taking any action.

- I have been advised of a potential Middle-Eastern buyer that might inject new equity into our company in return for a controlling state. It would seem that the British public does not object to such ownership when it comes to football clubs and stadiums, but does object to control of media outlets by such buyers. Where the public, and the government, stand on the ownership of utilities by a ~~foreign dictatorship~~ authoritarian government, remains to be seen.

I look forward to discussing these matters with the board, subject to unforeseen circumstances, in more detail at our meeting next week.

Jonathan Rolls
Acting Chief Financial Officer

19

EXILE: PAINTER

They often do not see me, even though I am standing right in front of them. There are a few reasons for this. I am an "artificer", a craftsman, and therefore beneath the notice of the lords and ladies whom I paint. I am a foreigner. My name is hard for them to pronounce and harder to spell: Marcus Gheeraerts. To some English especially hopeless with languages I am "Mark Gerard". I might have changed it, but in my trade having a Flemish surname has a certain cachet. They tend to assume that my English is poor, so sometimes during sketching sessions they say more in front of me than is strictly wise. The final layer of invisibility is that I am become old.

I look at my sitters more closely than they have ever been looked at before. A lover would soon blink. Their own children, bored, will quickly look away. But I have permission for an intricate examination. And I see their fears, their hopes. The court of her glorious majesty Elizabeth Regina was not an easy one in which to operate. Serving her successor King James is no less easy. So sometimes I espy apprehension, even fear. Sometimes pride. These feelings are mingled most evidently in the pregnancy portraits in which I have, strangely, become a specialist. The young wife is proud that she is hopefully about to produce the much-desired heir; her hand rests lightly on the bulge evident beneath her fine clothing. But I also often see the fear that she might lose the baby or die in childbirth. The portrait might prove to be both a celebration and epitaph. God knows, I know enough of this painful experience. My wife survives, but only two of our six children are still with us.

I fled from Bruges to London as a boy with my father when the Duke of Alva, may God damn his soul, was rounding up non-conformists. My mother was a Catholic, so we decided she should stay behind, to guard the shop pending our return. She died and we did not return. The "sect" to which my family and friends belong is called "*Huis der Liefde*"—the House of Love. Isn't that nice? We are a quiet group—we do not seek converts—but it means that our group of Dutch exiles here in the City of London is a tight one. My father remarried—Susanna de Critz, an exile from Antwerp. Strange to relate, I married my stepmother's sister, Magdalen. Our little circle includes quite a few artists—you may have heard of the poet Lucas de Heere? The map-maker Abraham Ortelius? There are also some successful merchants.

My breakthrough as a young man came when my talent was recognized by the Queen's Champion, Sir Henry Lee. He was in charge of the tilts organized each year to celebrate her majesty's accession to the throne. At first he had me painting decorations for the event on rolls of canvas, so can therefore claim to be behind the advance in technique which made my career. Portraits are mostly painted onto wood panels. By using lighter canvas I found I could paint huge, full-body portraits well suited to hang in the great hall of a baronial castle. I could fit whole families onto a single painting, allowing the lord to advertise both his fertility and confidence in continuation of the family line. My single most celebrated picture remains the one that Sir Henry had me paint to celebrate the visit of Queen Elizabeth to his home in Ditchley Oxfordshire. You know the one, with Gloria Regina resplendent in jewels bestriding England. If you look carefully, you will see that her toe is in Oxfordshire. Many copies were made. The original is now in Trinity College Cambridge. After that I had aristocratic families queueing up for me to take their likeness.

I have painted kings and queens, dukes and earls, distinguished foreign dignitaries, spies and traitors. Please do not imagine me standing behind a large easel. I work quickly. Once I have sketched the face and other important elements, the actual painting is done back at my workshop. I am now successful enough that I have a team who prime the canvas or oak boards – Baltic oak only please, the English stuff is too coarse grained and tends to warp. I always paint the face, hands and key details, but I have talented assistants to complete the background, the swags of satin curtains, the Turkish carpets or the upholstered chairs. I am fond of my workshop, which I share with my brother-in-law. I like the smell of oil and oak shavings, the sense of focussed activity and the rainbow shelves of pigments: lead white, lamp black, raw umber, red lead, vermillion, azurite and smalt.

The most dangerous customer I ever had was Robert Devereux, the Earl of Essex. The introduction came through his mother, who was a sister of Sir Henry Lee. He was the beau of his age and dashing courtier, most favoured of the Queen, until he wasn't. In my first portrait he asked that I show Cadiz burning in the background. I later learnt from a sailor that the raid achieved little, but Essex's portrait rewrote the story. After this I painted a veritable squadron of young braves, all trying to look as much like Essex as possible: beards cut square at the bottom, sleek bodices sharpening to a point above the family jewels. One hand rests negligently on the hilt of a sword, the other holds a medallion – the reward for bravery or religious keep-sake. If the noble had naval aspirations, I would paint a window through which could be seen a galleon tossing on a troubled sea. When Essex was undone by the Irish Wars and staged an ill-planned rebellion, many of these men followed him to the block. The one I felt most sorry for was Sir Henry's nephew, Captain Thomas Lee. He had me paint him as if on campaign in Ireland. He wished to be portrayed as the Roman hero Scaevola. It is the only chance I ever had to paint a man's naked legs.

You may ask how I escaped this debacle? Well, the old queen passed away shortly thereafter in her Richmond Palace. The new king, arriving weary and nervous from the deep north, was keen to demonstrate continuity. As much as possible should remain the same. He even had me paint his queen, Anne of Denmark, in the same fashions Elizabeth had worn, now archaic. Anne must have liked my portrait as I became "the Queen's Painter". The £79 I was paid for the set of four pictures of the King, Queen, Princess Elizabeth and Prince Charles was my best ever contract.

Every portrait painter must find the balance between realism and flattery. When dealing with princes this can be a sensitive matter. Should the wart be included? The crow's feet? Strangely, I have found older ladies most willing to accept reality; perhaps they have grown used to the skin which they inhabit. Young ladies are, less surprisingly, the hardest, paying inordinate attention to the minutest detail of jewellery and costume. For a high-born man the most important aspect to get correct is his heraldic achievement. Some had me accentuate a strategic war wound gained, of course, in their majesty's service. Prosperous merchants count my portraits successful if I can show just how expensive is the fur draped around their shoulders, and how intricate the crewel work on their wife's sleeve.

Clad in black, I followed Queen Anne's funeral procession. She was good to me. By that time, the court had already moved on to the latest generation of Flemish painters: van Somer, Mytens and so on. My work comes now from rural gentry—one asked me the other day to show him smiling! But I cannot complain. I have garnered a long career from my meagre talents in a tenuous profession. I can claim to have left my mark on this foreign land that cannot pronounce my name. The next time you are in a large house or castle, in a smoky hall, if there is a huge portrait on the wall, check in the corner for "MGF": *"Marcus Gheeraerts Fecit."*

20

Exile: KB

If you are reading this, I am dead.

I have often considered burning the attached documents. These are diaries from the 23 years during which I lived with Kaiser Wilhelm in exile in Holland. I fear that extracts from these documents will be used to criticise the Kaiser and the institution of the monarchy. This is not my intention. I was a Prussian officer of noble family and it was my duty, indeed honour, to serve his majesty. My dairies reflect some of the frustrations that such service entailed, but I have chosen not to censor them. At a time when so many are trying to re-write history, I believe that it is important to record these facts as I experienced them. I attach this note as a form of explanation.

It should be remembered that his majesty was already sixty when the catastrophe happened. I was there at the army HQ in Spa in Belgium at the start of November 1919 as our front lines started to collapse, and strikes intensified on the home front. It was then that the fateful decision was made for the Kaiser to "depart" for Holland. I quickly learnt not to use the word "flight"; it was always our "departure" or "journey" to Holland. This has since attracted much opprobrium, but I was there as the desperate alternatives were debated. One group of generals advocated rallying enough army units to take the Rhine bridges, march on Berlin and defeat the revolutionaries. There were questions, however, as to whether the army in its degraded state would accept orders to shoot their own countrymen. A civil war would only add to the grisly toll of the preceding five years. Another proposal was for the Kaiser and his sons to ride Götterdämmerung-style in a final charge against the enemy and die a glorious death worthy of a Hohenzollern. I do not believe that it was any lack of courage that this proposal was ruled out; apart from the Christian tenets against self-murder, the Kaiser felt that he still had a contribution to make to his country and his people. So it was decided that the least damaging way was for his majesty to stand aside to allow for a new government to be formed. His abdication was announced by the Chancellor in Berlin as a *fait accompli*, before it was approved by his majesty.

It is hard for a man of sixty years old, an autocrat used to having his orders obeyed immediately, to be suddenly stripped of power. After a hard night drive, we stopped at a place about fifty kilometres beyond the German border called Amerongen. Our host, Graf Bentinck, was "a real gentleman", an English phrase which the Kaiser must have used a hundred times. Despite regularly inveighing against the perfidious British Empire, which had allied with France and Russia to encircle Germany and cause the war, the Kaiser was strangely proud of his English heritage, as the eldest of Queen Victoria's grandsons. He often boasted to his children about his visits to England and how the old Queen had died in his arms.

The Kaiser would not be the only old man to repeat himself. The same phrases and stories would roll around. "My conscience is clear. God knows, I never wanted a war" was a favourite. The complicated "historical tables" attached were drawn up by the Kaiser to prove his innocence; what the Tsar said on a certain day; where the British fleet went on another day. How could he have been planning war when he was on an archaeology trip to Corfu in the early summer of 1914? When the Serbs sent that ultimatum to the Austrians, he was sailing in the Norwegian fjords.

The Kaiser is hardly the only man to have held political power that claims successes for himself but blame failures on others. Sometimes the objects of his condemnation are generic: it was the "limp-wristed civilians and Berlin Jews" who had stabbed the army in the back. Otherwise, it is specific individuals, no longer around to argue back, who were the objects of criticism: Ludendorff, Bethmann, Tirpitz, Bulow etc. etc. Long lost battles would be regularly refought with large maps spread across the dining table.

The Kaiser eventually bought his own house, Huis Doorn—a fine place, but located amidst the dismal, rain-soaked Dutch plains. He filled it with fifty wagon-loads of furniture and other personal items sent from Germany. One whole wagon was given over to uniforms. The endless, empty landscape of exile he filled with routine. At eight o'clock there was breakfast. Then a thorough examination of the German and Dutch papers; I intercepted them early and extracted the most incendiary articles, where possible. My preview of the mail would give me an indication of whether it was going to be a good day or a bad day. There would be a walk in the garden with his dog before lunch. After a post-prandial snooze, necessary documents would be attended to. Then the Kaiser would head out for exercise. In the old days, he was a keen hunter, slaughtering huge quantities of game, but the Doorn estate to which he was now restricted offered little such sport. So the Kaiser's favourite exercise became tree cutting. He cut down and sawed up a huge quantity of logs—more than we could ever burn. When we arrived, the Doorn estate was, fortunately, well wooded, but he left it completely shorn, like a plucked chicken. I sometimes would wonder aloud, during the lumberjack sessions, about the alternative pleasures of tree-planting. But why plant trees when he would shortly be recalled back to Germany, and restored to his rightful position, in order to sort out the terrible mess there?

The hardest times were the long evenings, sat in the smoking room, where he would eek out his two glasses of port wine, the second taken with water. Under a portrait of Frederick the Great, surrounded by family mementos of the glorious past, he would re-live old triumphs, as when he rode into Jerusalem in his white crusader uniform. More tediously, he would re-hash old defeats, and traduce reputations: how could President Wilson have allowed himself to be captured in that way by Lloyd George and Clemenceau? He would also develop ambitious plans, such as a joint Western crusade against "the Yellow Peril" in Asia, or "the Huns", as he called them. When the Kaiser eventually went to his bed, his final act was to place a loaded pistol on his bedside table. The Kaiser feared assassination or, worse, arrest, trial and humiliation by the Entente powers.

The Kaiser's children feature largely in the diaries. His majesty had six sons and one daughter, his favourite, Viktoria Luise. I have often been told that his majesty treated me as a son. The truth is that I had it much easier than his sons, who were kept on a short-lease, a function of the Kaiser's own strict upbringing. This perhaps contributed to the suicide of his youngest son, Joachim, and other scandals. Perhaps the most strained relationship was with his eldest, the Crown Prince Wilhelm, whom he normally referred to as "that young man". He was the only other member of the family restricted from returning to Germany. He had his own establishment in Holland on the desolate island of Wieringen. At the heart of the tension was the question, in the event of a restoration of the Hohenzollerns, would the people prefer an old man from a bygone era or a dashing, modern young prince. The

Crown Prince's wife, still based in a vast new palace in Potsdam, was his active lobbyist. The Kaiser's children themselves had between them nineteen children, so there were often youngsters around. His majesty probably derived more enjoyment from them than from his own children.

Visitors to Huis Doorn were generally a pleasant break from the frustrations of exile. Apart from family and friends, visitors consisted mostly of plotters or the merely curious. I did my best to screen out the inappropriate. If the Kaiser had a fault, I think it was his naivety in being willing to meet whoever he thought could help him back to his throne. I still shudder at the memory of the two visits by that terrible windbag Goring, with his knickerbockers and atrocious table manners. The Kaiser's wife, Augusta Victoria, had been a calming influence, and was much lamented when she sadly passed away in 1921, partly, I think, from homesickness. A hasty remarriage took place in the very next year. Princess Hermine Reuss von Greiz, a widow 29 years his junior, was much more ambitious. On her arrival, it was noticeable that the household retired use of the title "Kaiserin". The Kaiser, I think, understanding what he had lost, kept his first wife's room untouched, and visited it daily.

The Kaiser in exile was probably at his happiest when discussing archaeology with Professor Dorpfeld; his visits enlivened many evenings. The last time I saw the Kaiser truly happy was when the Wehrmacht swept into the Low Countries in 1940, just before his death. He welcomed the first squad to reach Doorn as "My soldiers" and invited them all to a fine breakfast. However, in the end he never allowed the National Socialists to use him to add lustre to their vulgar regime. Even when invited to return, a terrible temptation, he insisted he would never go back to a Germany without a restored monarchy. And so he lies buried at Doorn, in his favourite uniform, with the sleeve rucked up to disguise his withered left arm. It has since become a shrine to those who seek an earlier, alternative Germany.

Sigurd von Ilsemann

21

Exile: Chinese Gordon

Kunshan, 5th January 1864

Gentlemen,

I have received your letter of 23rd December. In answer to the same, I offer the following remarks confidentially, that you may bring your influence to bear in the appropriate quarters.

You find me at the headquarters of the Chinese Disciplined Force. I prefer to use this terminology rather than the more popular "Ever Victorious Army", which I know full well we are not. "Moderately Victorious Army" would be closer to the truth, though I understand the use of the former is better for the purposes of morale. It is true that I have withdrawn my co-operation with the Imperial forces after the outrage at Soochow. We secured capture of this well-fortified provincial capital with remarkably few casualties on my personal promise of safe conduct to the four "kings", that is to say commanders of the Taiping, that remained in the city. I was aware of dissension spreading amongst the rebel leaders and my promise was all that was required to unlock this prize. What do I find when I return to the city? Four bloody heads piled in a basket, and that arrant humbug Li Hongzhang gloating over them, having no doubt already dispatched a memorandum describing "his victory" to the Emperor.

You accuse me of "withdrawing to my tent like Achilles",

though, in this case, it is a pagoda. I am perfectly willing to resume command once I receive an apology from Governor Li. As Proverbs 12:22 states "The Lord detests lying lips." I have already rejected their blood money of 10,000 taels. I was tempted to accept and then use it for much needed medicines and provisions, but that would only confirm accusations about my "mercenary nature". I am not here for the money. A simple letter of apology will suffice.

I hope that the "Foreign United Defence Bureau" feels that it has got its money's worth since it appointed me to lead this force last March? The force has never numbered more than 4000 men, a fraction of enemy numbers, and these men were largely deserters from the rebel cause, led by a bunch of foreign adventurers. But I have no complaint about their bravery. It is amazing how men respond to proper pay, arms, discipline and food; the stomach governs the world. Opium addicts are, of course, summarily dismissed and hard liquor banned. This done, I assess the quality of these troops as higher than that of the Indian Army sepoys I have fought alongside. It was fortunate that I was engaged in surveying the Yangtze delta before being appointed to command. Knowledge of its labyrinth of canals and lakes has been vital to the speed of our success. This and our "navy". It has never amounted to more than two small paddle steamers that would be mocked by any self-respecting admiral. But the key is that they were armoured, carried a 32lb cannon and drew only 4 feet. This has allowed us swiftly to bring firepower to bear on any rebel fortifications. I believe that my strategy of outflanking manoeuvres to cut communications and surprise attacks, rather than previously favoured frontal assaults, has also saved lives.

I appreciate your expression of concern for my safety and instructions not to expose myself "so rashly" to enemy fire. I can assure you that, when entering action, I am frightened, usually very much so. But I am not frightened of death; the Lord has numbered the hairs on my head and knows when I will die. I am frightened of failure and disgrace. I advance into battle armed only with a swagger stick because it is not my job to kill rebels personally, but to direct my men to victory. I know the men believe my stick to possess some strange magic and have taken to calling it my "Victory Wand", but if it helps their morale and hurts that of the foe, where is the harm? Of course, I have killed men, such as the ring-leader of a mutiny here just three months ago. He had to be executed and I had to be seen to do it, but I derive no pleasure from such things.

There is nothing like a civil war to bring out the beast in man. I have already travelled more of the world than most men and seen some horrid sights—from the ramparts at Sevastopol, amongst the flames of the Summer Palace. But I have never seen anything as grim as the trail of skeletal corpses we follow on our advance. Just because the so-called "Heavenly King" claims to be the younger brother of Jesus Christ, I have been accused of fighting on behalf of Buddhists against Christians. There is nothing Christian about the Taipings. That sinner will be called to answer for all the poor, bloodied children I have seen, and soon. "Better for him if a millstone were hung around his neck and he be cast into the sea."

This rebellion will be finished within six months (D.V.). Shanghai is, I believe, already safe. It will be tempting to demobilize the Force immediately. I beg for you to take care. The sudden emptying onto your streets of men trained to kill and devoid of new employment will not go well. You will also need to consider carefully how to treat those foreigners fighting for the rebels, who will soon be approaching you to plead for mercy. As for me, I would be grateful if you could use your influence to find me another active appointment; a general's metier is in the field not the office. I do not need reward. The yellow robe, peacock feather and medallions that I am awarded by the Emperor will fit easily into my kit bag. The British Empire is broad; there must be some trouble somewhere that needs attending to. Perhaps there is something in the Middle East? I would love to see Jerusalem before I die What I would hate is to return to London, with its wearisome dinner parties, having to talk to women, saying what I do not mean, and eating and drinking what I do not want. Better a ball in the brain than to flicker out unheeded in such social dalliance.

With appreciation for your assistance.

Yours sincerely,

C.E. Gordon

Note: in 1896 Li Hongzhang, on his visit to London, laid a wreath at the statue of Major General Gordon in Trafalgar Square. This statue of "Gordon of Khartoum", clutching a bible, with swagger stock under his arm, has now been demoted to the Victoria Embankment. The abbreviation D.V., with which Gordon's letters are liberally strewn, stands for "Deo Volente". God willing.

22

STATUES

Dear Dad,
I hope you are keeping well? I am sorry I haven't been over to see you recently, but Martha hasn't got any more holidays left this year. Perhaps we'll fly over early next year, when it gets warmer, but before the Easter holidays push up the price of tickets.

I attach something I have written. I am not sure it's your cup of tea, but I didn't know who else to send it to—I don't want to let it just sit in a drawer. At least it might bring back some memories for you of the old town. You will see that you, Mum, West Ham United and Grandad all get a mention! Best not to say anything about it to Martha, for reasons you'll see. But don't worry about me—I'll be fine.

I won't talk about football—surely they have to change the manager soon?

Love
Ron x

Statues of London
I didn't notice them until I was fired. It was a tough time for the City. Another financial crisis. All of the investment banks were "down-sizing" their trading teams. So, I was "let go", as they say. FIFO. First in, first out. I'd been on the desk for a few years, and was pulling down a decent wage, so represented a

significant cost-saving. LIFO would only have only harvested a bunch of graduate trainees on slave wages (by investment bank standards, anyway).

Maybe it was for the best. They'd always made fun of me. Not so much for coming from Romford—there are plenty of Essex boys on City trading desks—but more for reading books, during my breaks and when the markets were quiet. History books. They wouldn't have said anything if I'd been reading the sports pages of the Mail. Or doom-scrolling through social media (as if I didn't get enough of screens all day). Or if I headed off to the gym, to come back all sweaty with a virtuous glow. I like history - a chance to understand another world, to live another life. I have no time for fiction, some made-up characters falling in-and-out of love or solving unlikely crimes. So I went from "Romford Ronnie" to "Ronnie the Egghead". My hair is thinning—no big deal.

The thing is, I haven't told my wife yet. It's a bit embarrassing. She always made fun of my job—"just pushing money about". There is more to derivatives trading than that, but you are never going to win an argument about social worth with a nurse. I didn't hear her complaining about all the money I made. So now I set off and come back at the normal time. It's not so bad. The bank had already allowed some working-from-home before I left, which I use sparingly. Also, it's not like I have to wear a pin-striped suit and tie. The bank would never let me within a mile of a client, so comfortable sweatshirt and chinos are the norm. All this means that I have plenty of spare time in central London. That's when I started "collecting" statues.

I make a list, and tick them off. I take a selfie with each statue. I mostly walk—good for the beer belly - but I sometimes rent a bike if the statue is far away. On days when the weather is poor, I head to the library to read up on who they were. I have a British

Library reader's ticket. It's really convenient and doesn't cost me anything. Also the library canteen offers a good deal on lunch - £4.10 for a nourishing soup and bread!

I've already collected over 300 statues. It doesn't involve as much walking as you might think. They're concentrated in Westminster. There aren't many statues in the City, which suits me fine. I wouldn't want to bump into any of my old team mates. Sure, I miss the banter, the gallows humour, but I wouldn't know what to talk about, now that I am not part of it all. I've got my eye out for new opportunities, of course, but no one's hiring at the moment. These things go in cycles. Anyway, I have built up some savings and got a decent pay-off, so we'll be all right for a while. Meanwhile, London has plenty of statues for me to visit.

Given London's long history, you'd expect its statues to date from an extended period, but it's not true. If you only count public statues - out in the open for anyone to see, not in churches or museums - I guess a 50-year period, 1870 to 1920, would bag at least half of the total statue population. This was the height of empire, when society had self-confidence and the will-power to celebrate it. Erecting a public statue is not easy. The backstories are full of problems raising money, arguments about selection of artist, disagreement about the proposed design and, finally, the difficulty of finding a suitable location. The biggest demand for statues seems to come at the end of wars, which mostly coincide with an economic slump. The government, its resources depleted, bleats and havers about honouring "the glorious dead". I'm not going to talk about war memorials here. It is too depressing, especially those for one war which get re-used for the next. WWII names get crammed into a small space below the scroll of WWI dead. Then there's a small plaque added on later for Korea. My name is amongst the fallen in Romford Town Hall. But then I am named after my great-grandfather, the hero.

The motivation behind building most of London's statues can be summed up as either gratitude, obligation or guilt. There is little in the way of Ancient Egyptian-style self-glorification. Ironically, the oldest public monument in London, much older than London itself, is the so-called Cleopatra's needle. This "gift" from a grateful Egyptian government actually boasts the virtues of Thutmose III (1458 to 1425 BC), or "the Great" as he liked to be known. In a gloomily inappropriate site, far from the desert sands of Egypt, he has sat by the side of the Thames for over a hundred years as London's acid rain gradually leaches away his achievements.

English kings and queens unsurprisingly make up a significant part of the statue cohort—Stuarts, Hanoverians and Battenbergs (sorry "Windsors"—well you wouldn't want to be named after a cake, would you?). Queen Victoria is by far the most heavily represented, as you might expect, given that she was in place for a long time right at the apogee of imperial glory. She is unusual in having been present at the unveiling of her own statue. In almost all other cases, being dead is a minimum qualification. Although in 2007 Nelson Mandela did attend the unveiling of his own statue, squeezed uncomfortably into one corner of Parliament Square. South African prime minister Smuts, a supporter of apartheid, has a much better central spot, and is shown striding confidently forward, past the glowering hulk of Churchill, whom he once interrogated as a young man during the Boer war. Whereas obligation (i.e. toadying) probably accounts for most royal statues, guilt is the reason that Charles I is the next most represented monarch. His statue on a horse, apparently the oldest of its kind in London, now faces down Whitehall to his place of execution. There is also a rather sheepish bust of Charles on the end of St. Margaret's church. He peers out at, horror of horrors, the statue of his nemesis, Oliver Cromwell, who stands hard by the walls of Parliament, which he dissolved not once but twice! Even to a boy from Billericay, it seems astonishing that a man who eventually set himself up as military dictator should be so honoured by the "mother of democracies". Unsurprisingly, opposition from Irish MPS was particularly fierce, given the number of Catholics Cromwell massacred. So Lord Rosebery was left to fund his proposal himself, helped by his wife, a Rothschild heir. He said that Cromwell was the first English "monarch" to be kind to the Jews…

I don't go to church much myself. Occasionally my wife drags me along on one of the important holy days or to a wedding. I prefer old churches, where there's more to see, flags and monuments carved with skulls and such. Also I am not averse to a rousing hymn, as long as it is one of the famous ones. I also admit to having prayed now and then, though not usually in church, but when I am in trouble. On that terrible flight over Siberia. Or when that Yen swap deal went against me, big time.

Richard Coeur de Lion occupies pride of place at the entrance to Parliament. It is a fine statue by a man called Baron Marochetti, with the armoured knight holding his sword triumphantly aloft. But Richard was a terrible king! Of his 10-year reign he spent about 6 months in England. He fought both his father and brother, usually in alliance with the King of France (boooo…). He drained the country's resources to pay for a crusade which, despite victories in battle, failed to capture Jerusalem, although he was twice within sight of it. On his way out, Richard launched unscheduled invasions of Sicily and Cyprus. On the way back home, he allowed himself to be captured by Leopold of Austria, so forcing his poor subjects to pay his ransom. After his release, the ungrateful bastard proceeded to get himself shot by a crossbow at an unnecessary siege of a nowhere castle in the Perigord and die of gangrene. What a fine role model for Parliament to choose.

I sometimes eat a PRET smoked salmon sandwich in the park in St. James Square. There's a library there where I read the FT and Economist for free and keep up with markets. In the centre of the park is a statue of William III. I don't know whether the park committee were aware of the irony that it was protestant William who pushed Catholic James off the throne in the "Glorious Revolution" then defeated him at the Battle of the Boyne. There is another statue of "Stinking Billy", as he is affectionately known in Ireland, in Kensington Gardens, which was a gift by Kaiser Wilhelm to his nephew, Edward VII. You can imagine the conversation "Oh, thank you very much Willie, just what I wanted. Another statue." An embarrassing statue of James II himself, relocated several times, finally came to rest in front of the National Gallery. The sculptor has dressed him as a Roman, which makes it look as though he has been caught on his way back from a toga party. Before I leave the subject of royal statues, I must mention the blingiest of all—the Albert Memorial in Hyde Park. Here sits Queen Victoria's consort, coated in 24 carat gold. This OTT, somewhat phallic monument surely puts in question Victoria's famous lack of humour. They had nine children together before Albert died, worn out, at the age of just 42. She missed him—I get it. Martha and me haven't had any children—yet. We always agreed we were too busy. Now I've got time but...I hardly see myself as a house-husband. I can empty a dishwasher, and make a decent sausage sandwich, but as for changing diapers and stuff. I used to see new fathers on my team shuffle in looking like extras from a zombie movie. It would be all right when the little chap can run about, play football. I'd be good at that.

Out-numbering even the royals, the biggest brigade of statues is generals. Wellington is the best represented. He also lived to see his statue unveiled—there's a good one in front of the Bank of England. But even Wellington could be the victim of fashion. A massive equestrian statue of him was lifted to the top of the victory arch on Constitution Hill in 1847, but was eventually thought such an eyesore it was taken down and banished to Aldershot. Its replacement is a chariot with four maddened horses, driven by a figure meant to represent "Peace" who looks anything but peaceful. The other famous chariot statue is, of course, of the revolting Boadicea. She is shown charging into battle against the Romans with two inappropriately-clad daughters and no reins to control her horses. Rarely can a city so celebrate a person who burnt it to the ground. The statue was donated by the family of the sculptor, Thomas Thornycroft, after his death. I guess it was cluttering up the garden shed.

Probably London's most famous statue, certainly the most elevated—Nelson's column - took twenty-eight years to build. It was not finished until 1867, sixty-two years after the admiral died at the moment of a victory which secured for Britain a naval superiority which enabled the empire. The empty "fourth plinth" in Trafalgar Square was originally intended to feature William IV, to accompany his brother George IV, but the money ran out. It is now occupied by a different sculpture each year, selected by competition. The other two plinths are occupied by the hirsute Sir Charles Napier and Sir Henry Havelock, respectively, names which most Londoners, including our mayor, cannot identify. What links these obscure generals with a veritable platoon of others along the Victoria Embankment (Outram, Campbell, Roberts) apart from fine moustaches, is service in India. A large number were involved in the Indian Mutiny, a sort of Imperial heart attack, which prompted a surge in statue-building by a grateful elite to those that saved their bacon.

Trafalgar Square is a good place to watch people reacting to statues. There are stone benches and, if you like, you can pretend to be feeding the pigeons. Visitors look up, not that you can see much of Nelson from that angle. (For the record, he is accurately shown with one empty sleeve, but is missing his eye-patch). The statues of the other old, white men are ignored. Far more attention is given to the fine bronze Landseer lions at the base of the column, which daring children, bored by whole day of sight-seeing, are keen to climb.

In an era of "cancel culture", where the statue of a slave-owner can be rolled into Bristol harbour, and institutions sponsored by the beneficiaries of slavery indulge in lengthy self-criticism, it is surprising how some of London's statues survive. Indian visitors to the Foreign Ministry must still squeeze past the statue of "Clive of India", whose victories helped win India for the empire, earned him a vast fortune, and contributed to the great Bengal famine. Perhaps there is some karmic justice in knowing that he eventually stabbed himself in the neck with a paper knife. "Bomber Harris", or "Butcher Harris" as he was known to his men, was the leading proponent of area bombing in World War II. He still stands to attention outside St. Clement Danes Church on the Strand. It is not surprising that the mayors of Cologne (objective of his first 1000-bomber raid in 1942) or Dresden (an estimated 25,000 dead in the 1945 firestorm), vainly objected to its unveiling.

One character whom I initially thought ripe for cancelling or downgrading is Field Marshall the Right Honourable the Lord Napier of Magdala GCB GCSI FRS. He sits on his horse at the top of Queens Gate, in solar topee, holstered pistol and binoculars in hand. He faces Hyde Park, looking slightly to his right, so he can see the Albert Memorial when the leaves fall. He was present at not one but two imperial pillages—the burning of the Summer Palace in Peking and the sack of the Ethiopian fortress of Magdala. The Ethiopian silver collection still sits in the nearby Victoria & Albert Museum. To see his Summer Palace loot you need to go to the Royal Engineers Museum in Chatham (Note: it is best not to use the word "loot" in front of the curator, or "restitution"). However, the more I read about him, the more sympathetic I become. His soldier father died of wounds shortly after this birth. Signed up to the army when 16, he was himself wounded at the Battle of Ferozeshah, again at the siege of Multan and again in the relief of Lucknow. After the assault on the Taku Forts, he found six bullet holes through his clothing. There is no evidence that he benefitted personally from looting. Having survived cholera and dysentery in his Indian campaigns, he eventually succumbed to influenza in his London home having fathered 15 children. Perhaps he deserved his state funeral and statue.

There are some military leaders for whom it is less easy to feel sympathy. The main achievement of "Gentlemen Johnny" Burgoyne, now standing on Carlton Terrace, was to surrender his entire army at Saratoga in the American War of Independence. He later eloped with the daughter of Lord Derby and went on to be an MP. I have worked with a few "Gentlemen Johnnys" at the Bank. There are tell-tale signs even before they open their mouths—red braces or patterned waistcoat, striped socks, polished black brogues. The parade of WW1 generals down Whitehall is also hard to like. Occupying prime spot is the polo-playing, Bullingdon Club man The Earl Haig, described by a colleague as "humourless and inflexible", under whose command on the Western Front (1915-18) his men suffered two million casualties.

Statues exude an aura of permanence, but it is surprising

how often London's statues move around. This is sometimes a function of changes in road or rail lay-outs as the city developed. The iconic statue of Eros, innovatively cast in aluminium to honour the 7th Earl of Shaftesbury for his crusade against child exploitation, was moved once for the remodelling of Picadilly station then again for safety during WWII. The removal of some statues, however, reflects a change in attitude towards the person once celebrated. Major General Gordon's statue was unveiled in a prime site in Trafalgar Square in 1888, a mere three years after his death in Khartoum, as Prime Minister Gladstone suddenly went from GOM (Grand Old Man) to MOG (Murderer of Gordon). The statue of a pensive Gordon holding a bible and swagger stick has subsequently been relegated to an anonymous site on the embankment. He is now within a spear's throw of an odd memorial to the Imperial Camel Corp, which had already been disbanded by the time the statue was unveiled. Some statues have left only a name: King's Cross station is named after a memorial to George IV that was so ugly it was demolished.

Sometimes alterations are made after unveiling. On the exuberant Monument to the Fire of London, wording which blames it on Papists was removed under James II, re-inserted under William III, then removed again in 1830. The government made much in its propaganda of the execution by Germany in 1915 of the nurse Edith Cavell, found guilty of smuggling allied prisoners to safety. Her statue, built with a subscription from loyal readers of the Telegraph, was topped by the patriotic slogan "For King and Country". Four years later, at the insistence of the National Council of Women, Cavell's final words were added, completely undermining this fatuous sentiment: "Patriotism is not enough. I must have no hatred or bitterness towards anyone."

There are not many statues of women, royalty aside. My wife would be pleased that three of the most prominent are of nurses. Apart from Nurse Cavell's memorial cited above, there is the statue of Florence Nightingale holding the wrong type of lamp, added in 1915, five years after her death, to the Crimean War memorial. Her fame reflects guilt for a war which achieved nothing, but cost 750,000 casualties, many from disease. The memorial itself is cast from "cannons captured at Sevastopol", as though that makes a difference. Florence's contemporary, Mary Jane Seacole, who dispensed medical assistance and provisions from her British Hotel in the Crimea, had to wait till 2016 for her impressive if ugly statue to be unveiled at St. Thomas' Hospital. Mother Seacole's cheerfulness in adversity and her ability to talk to all ranks, shines through in her auto-biography—apparently the first to be published by a black woman in the U.K. I would have liked a mother like Mary. I am not dissing my own mother, but she died when I was so young. I realize my memories of her are just patched together from old photos and my Dad's stories. I have even found myself looking for her features in the female statues. I admit it's a bit odd. What am I looking for? The Romford Madonna?

In an effort to address the gender imbalance, statues were recently unveiled to two attractive young female spies, both members of the SOE France section—Violette Szabo on the Albert Embankment and Noor Inayat Khan in Bloomsbury. Virginia Woolf also warrants one statue in Bloomsbury and another on Richmond Riverside. This latter is an example of the growing and regrettable trend to "What's App" statues, where you can sit with them on a bench and take a selfie. "Look, I'm with Viriginia and was able to finish at least ten pages of "To the Lighthouse"".

There are few statues of bald men. Receding hairlines are common, but total slapheads are rare. Clearly there is some cheating with hats and, especially in the 18th century, wigs. So far, I have counted only John Stuart Mills and Sigmund Freud, but you expect your philosophers and psychologists to be bald. There is Gandhi in Parliament Square, of course, who has both bare head and legs. On my last visit, he was looking especially cold and miserable, tucked into some damp London shrubbery and crowned with pigeon shit. Who was it said posterity is having pigeons shit on your head for ever? Next to Gandhi, and different from him in almost every way, stands Lord Palmerston ("Change? Aren't things bad enough already?"), who wins the prize for best side-burns. Perhaps I should grow a moustache and beard, to compensate? Too cliched? Too hipster?

Artists are poorly represented. I am pleased that both Gilbert and Sullivan have memorials not far from each other on the Embankment. My Mum used to like their shows; I once took her to see "The Mikado" at the Brookside. Not far from Gilbert & Sullivan, on Horseguard's Parade, is Field Marshal Garnet Wolseley, Gilbert's very model of a "Modern Major General" in the operetta "Pirates of Penzance". Apparently, Wolseley used to sing it at parties. Of the poets, apart from Shakespeare (who qualifies in the "almost bald" category) there is Keats, hiding in the garden at Guy's Hospital, where he trained to be a surgeon. The infamous Byron statue, subject of the longest libel trial ever to be heard at Westminster Hall, has now been consigned to an inaccessible traffic island at the bottom of busy Park Lane. Now Byron is not only mad and bad, but also dangerous to visit. A young Mozart fiddles away in Orange Park (he lived in nearby Ebury Road when he was eight, which seems a weak excuse). In Victoria Park, near a good kebab stall, sponsored by Westminster Council, the composer Purcell has been re-envisioned as an explosion.

Businessmen and engineers get short shrift. Perhaps the most deserving is the statue to Joseph Bazalgette, the engineer responsible for London's sewage system, several Thames bridges and the very embankment where he now resides. Plimsoll has a nice memorial nearby paid for by the National Union of Seamen, to whose safety his work on ship marking contributed. There are no statues of bankers. Well, there are, but it is always in the context of what they did with their money – build a hospital, set up Sunday schools etc. The only statue to a financial speculator I found was Thomas Guy, who stands in the courtyard of Guy's Hospital, which he built with the proceeds of selling shares in the South Sea Company, the meme coins of their day, before the bubble burst.

There are surprisingly few statues to sporting heroes. My favourite is the one of Bobby Moore by Upton Park celebrating when West Ham won the World Cup in 1966. All right, England won the cup, but it was the West Ham players in the team that made the difference. I used to go and watch the football with Dad, before he moved to the South of Spain. The Hammers' latest game is now the main topic of our weekly phone call. There is a statue to someone who can claim to be the original celebrity – someone famous just for being famous. Beau Brummel, dandy and one-time favourite of the Prince Regent, swaggers outside Picadilly Arcade. What the statue does not state, but perhaps should as a salutary warning, is that gambling debts forced him to flee to France, where he died in an asylum of syphilis. I don't gamble – unless I have inside information, of course. Anyone with the vaguest grasp of maths knows that the House wins. My prolonged walks around London reveal that the fastest growing type of high street store, after charity shops, is bookies. It's depressing to see guys slinking into these pokey stores, then pissing what little money they have up against the wall. It wasn't gambling that got me fired.

New statues continue to be unveiled, though we lack the confidence of our Victorian forebears. Which of the current crop of politicians, artists and celebrities will be deemed worthy of a London statue? Keir Starmer in Highbury Fields? A gift from the U.S. of a statue of Donald Trump, perhaps posed in a golf cart, squeezing aside the earlier gift of Abraham Lincoln? My vote goes for David Attenborough, standing by the gates of Richmond Park, with the planet in his hands. Or perhaps a statue of Sarah Gilbert, who led the push for the Oxford vaccine, holding a hypodermic over the Covid wall opposite Parliament? Who gets your vote?

Don't worry about me. I'll find something before my wife twigs. Maybe I'll sign up as mature student for a history course and earn my nickname. In my spare time I can lead tours of London's statues: look out for "Egghead Tours".

23

Meaning

The green neon letters told Ben that it was 7:32, just as they had successively told him it was 2:33, 4:26 and 5:57. His wife rolled over onto her back; she wasn't snoring you understand, just breathing loudly. Even though it was a Sunday, this was a not an unreasonable time to get up. The local corner shop, run by the nice couple from Nepal, would be open by the time he was showered and dressed. The owner was an ex-Gurkha who still kept military hours. Anyway, the alarm would wake his wife at 7:45, when she would rouse their daughter to start piano practice. After that, Rachmaninoff and Beethoven would decisively prevent any further sleep.

As he prepared to leave, he picked up purse and keys, and shouted: "I'm going to get a newspaper. Anyone want anything?". The corner shop was small with a limited offering of foodstuffs, mostly unhealthy and long-life. The piano music paused temporarily for a cry of "White Monster!" He recognised this as a low-sugar but highly caffeinated beverage preferred by his daughter when she felt underpowered.

It was only about 500 metres to the corner shop—one of the benefits of living in central London. There was not usually much call for social interaction before he reached it, when some brief banter on the recent fortunes and prospects of Arsenal football club would be exchanged. He sometimes got a wave from the nightwatchman, when the friendly Barbadian was on duty. Occasionally, if he was up early enough, he saw an urban fox returning to its lair or was squawked at by the brightly coloured parakeets which, far from their native jungle, now sped like cruise missiles over Pimlico. There was also the odd dog walker, proudly swinging his green bag of faeces.

But the person now approaching him was looking at him directly, rather than averting his eyes or consulting his iPhone. This was against the rules. He wondered whether he should cross the street. Too late.

"Excuse me." Chinese tourist by the look of it. Still in his 20s, dark complexion, straggly moustache and goatee. Backpack.

"I'm lost."

This should be all right. He had lived here for a few years already. He would be able to direct a misplaced tourist towards Westminster Abbey or Buckingham Palace.

"Where would you like to go?" Ben asked, politely.

"No, I meant I'm lost. I am looking for … meaning."

There was a bemused pause as he considered possible near homonyms: Manning Street? Mannering Park? Noticing his confusion, the would-be tourist continued.

"I am looking for the meaning … of life".

The slightest of smirks could be seen beneath the straggly beard, and Ben realised he was being played. Well, it was Sunday, and he was in no rush. Finally, his much-mocked degree in Oriental Studies would come in useful.

"I see. That's certainly a tricky one. I guess you are coming from China?"

There was a nod of agreement.

"In that case, you might like to start with the classics—Confucius for ethics, where the meaning of life is doing the right thing. A father should act in a fatherly way to his son, and his son in a filial way to his father and so on. Then there is Laozi and Chuangzi for metaphysics, where one should follow nature as a way to achievement. For rules, regulations and strategy, perhaps Han Feizi and Sunzi. Then there's Neo-Confucian Wang Yangming, for putting into effect what you learn - the unity of knowledge and action."

The meaning-of-life-tourist had lost his smirk.

"I don't want old books."

"Oh, you mean modern Chinese philosophy? There's Sun Yat-sen's Three Principles, which is still popular in Taiwan. Or Mao Zedong, of course, where the meaning of life lies in serving the people. I know Xi Jinping has recently made some valuable contributions on the subject, but I'm sorry to admit that I haven't yet got round to reading them. It would be easier for you—I am sure his books are more exciting in the original."

The tourist smiled as he saw an escape route.

"Well, thank you for your suggestions. I see this is a matter in which you have interest. You clearly have had a longer time than me to study it". He was looking at my grey hair and wrinkles. "What is your conclusion?"

"It's Sunday. Just along this road are several churches where, I am sure, they would be eager to share their answers with you. There's even a mosque. I don't know of any Buddhist temples nearby, but all that 'escape from the veil of tears' stuff always struck me as rather dismal."

"So you have come to no conclusion yourself about meaning? What about death?"

"Oh, I'm strictly in the 'bones and silence' camp. You may live on in the minds of friends and relatives for a short while. Perhaps your memory will survive a little longer if you have created something good—an interesting book, stirring music, a fine building or a successful business. That's the end of it, I think."

"Well, it's been nice talking to you."

The tourist offered his hand, which was strangely hard and blistered for a young man. Then, with a valedictory wave, he walked way. His New York Yankees baseball cap sat at an odd angle, thanks to two strange protuberances at the base of his skull.

Ben continued to the shop. He paid for the Observer and a can of Monster with a swipe of his debit card.

"So how do you think the Man City match will go this afternoon?"

24

Exile: Spy

You'll think I am a traitor. Especially if you are a certain kind of Englishman. "Scholarship to Westminster. Trinity College. How could you?" I went up to Cambridge, full of those socialist ideas of equality and liberty that every young man should have, just as the economic crisis of 1931 was made worse by the "National Government". I then watched as the democracies bought the empty promises of Fascists. What right-thinking young man at that time would not find the utopian goals of Karl Marx attractive? Work for SIS in the war then catapulted me into the higher ranks of the intelligence service. The rest, as they say, is history, albeit a redacted history in my case.

The first few years after my defection in 1963 were the hardest. The KGB were not sure to do with me, so I had a lot of time on my hands. I have never sought the company of other expatriates. I hate the wining and dreary exchange of nostalgia, the exile's drug-of-choice. I avoided journalists. They provided me with a decent pension—500 roubles per month, raised to 800 recently—and a quiet flat in an alley off Pushkin Square in central Moscow. It was lonely. I kept a low profile, living under an assumed name. My first surname was Fyodorov, but my Russian remains lamentable, so this was difficult to carry off. My cover was changed to that of a Latvian scientist, so now I only have to fear meeting a fellow Latvian.

What saved me was finding a local, younger wife. Her mother is Polish, so she is not entirely native, but her circle of friends is much wider than mine. I also learnt about "*blat*" — how to make use of connections. I learnt the importance of my access to the Beryozka foreign currency store. The KGB found work for me to do. I have now taught several classes of recruits on how to socialize, what to wear and how to carry themselves to fit into society in the West. I hear your spluttering outrage "But can't you see the iniquities of the Soviet System?" Every week I go over to the main Post Office to collect a week's worth of copies of the Times, Sunday Times and Herald Tribune. I keep up with the antics of that ignorant clown Reagan and his poodle Mrs. T. I watch them enrich the wealthy, immiserate the poor and indulge in imperialist ventures in the Middle East, Asia and South America. So don't wag your fingers at me. They may spin you a good line about "free speech" and "democracy" but open your eyes to what is actually happening. I accept that my apartment is bugged and my mail read, and so censor myself accordingly. How secure is your communication? It is shocking how much is revealed by those blissfully unaware they are being overheard. You should trust me on this one — I am well-placed to judge.

It has been written that I have a fondness for the bottle, a hazard of my profession, it seems. I never touch spirits until 6pm, and then limit myself to two glasses. Whisky or brandy of preference. There may also be the odd dry red wine to wash down lunch or a restorative hair-of-the-dog-that-bit-you in cases of emergency. However, unlike some of my brethren, I am not an angry drunk. I may admittedly lose something in the way of intelligibility. My wife has taken to diluting my drinks and hiding the bottles, but what kind of spy would I be if I could not arrange counter-measures. At her request, I have stopped smoking in the bedroom — she objected to burn-marks on the bedclothes, and now limit myself to one pack per day. I prefer Gauloises or Gitanes when I can get them—I worry about the health effect of filters—but make do with Dymok or Prima if there is no alternative.

My schedule is regular. At 7am I will be seated by my radio to listen to the BBC World Service, whilst drinking two or three cups of tea with aspirins. I might listen to British broadcasts, but I drink my tea as a Russian with lemon. For breakfast I like toast, preferably with Oxford Coarse Cut Marmalade; visiting children or students back from postings know to bring me fresh supplies. Other items on the list to be smuggled in are a good Maille Mustard and various spices for curry—I like a good curry, so now must make them for myself. The food here is generally acceptable; I have a strong stomach. I have learnt in stores to buy more of something if I like it, in case it is not there next time. My cupboards at home are filled with tins against possible shortages; I am currently very long of tuna-in-tomato-sauce.

After breakfast, we often take a stroll along Tverskoy Boulevard before my wife has to rush off to her work at the publishing house. In the evenings I like to watch TV. My weak Russian hampers my understanding of drama, but I like sports, especially football. No team could replace my beloved Arsenal of course, but for convenience's sake here I have adopted Dynamo. In the summer, I can only follow the ups-and-downs of Surrey Cricket Club at a distance in the Times. My favourite feature in the paper is the cryptic crossword.

You may think me trapped in my golden cage in Moscow, but I travel extensively. I have enjoyed summer trips to Siberia—especially Irkutsk and Lake Baikal. Mostly, however, because of my bronchitis, we head south to the Black Sea; the Sunshine Shore in Bulgaria is a particular favourite.

I am not sure how many years I have left. I am reconciled

to a quiet funeral in a Moscow cemetery. At the service, I have requested my favourite song—"My Way". My children come out from England, usually once per year, which is nice. They come with various spouses and grand-children. My notoriety does not seem to have ruined their lives. My children see more of me than I ever saw of my father. He was in the Indian Civil Service, so I was packed to boarding school when still very young—an early black mark against the British Empire. At my age you start to question the life choices that you made. What would it have been like to rise up quietly through MI6, live in Tunbridge Wells, spend afternoons at the Oval and the occasional week-end shooting in the Borders or fishing on the Test? I doubt I would have been happier. When I look at the consolidated profit and loss account, I believe I have done more good than wrong. But I would say that, wouldn't I?

25

Evening Ferry

Good. The boat was at the wharf, so he wouldn't need to wait long. He flipped the plastic entry token into a basket and hurried down the broad gangplank, coat flapping. Actually he was not in a rush. He rarely was these days; business was quiet. It's just that he did not want the gate to slam shut right in front of his face. The muddy river slid unappetisingly beneath the gaps in the steel. The surface was slippery so his manly stride became an undignified waddle. Still, better that than a pratfall before the eyes of those already aboard. Carefully minding the gap, he climbed aboard.

It was rush-hour in one of the world's largest cities, but the crowd on the ferry was thin. A two-decade building boom had criss-crossed the Huangpu River with several rival bridges and tunnels to nudge the old ferry towards obsolescence. Growing wealth had bought a surge in car ownership—a warmer and more convenient transport alternative on this cool evening in early spring. He remembered his first ride on this ferry thirty years before. It had been packed with people pushing bicycles or motorbikes, many of them heavily-laden. Once he had even seen a pig strapped across a handlebars. Now his fellow travellers seemed mostly to be local tourists. They were not the cap-wearing, flag-following tourists of yore; this too had changed. These ones, dressed in sports-leisure clothes, lined the top deck, taking pictures of each other and Pudong's towering skyscrapers. After a few minutes, a man in a New York Yankees cap lost interest in his surroundings, re-inserted his earphones and started flicking through his WeChat messages. On his first trip, he had only taken the ferry to take a picture of the famous colonial architecture along the West bank, "the Bund". He had stayed on the boat when it turned around—there had been nothing on the East side of the river worth getting off for. This photograph, rather faded, was still pinned above his desk. The old 1920's skyline that it showed was now lost, dwarfed by the work of a new generation of empire builders.

At least the ferry still smelled the same; a hint of the sea over engine oil and an ammonia-based cleaning fluid. Also unchanged was the practised ease with which the blue-clad sailor un-looped the rope from its stanchion and cast off into the stream. The propellers suddenly churned against the tide and he pressed his hand against a cabin window to steady himself. He caught his own reflection and was startled to see how much he stood out, in his grey suit, long raincoat and dark glasses. "Daddy, look, it's an old foreigner." The child was quickly shushed by his father and distracted with something more interesting—a passing barge named "Struggle 281" heaped with sand.

He could have taken a taxi, of course, but his office looked right across the river at the club where the lecture was taking place. Even considering the ferry's leisurely pace, the taxi would not have been any quicker, having tunnel traffic to contend with. Also, after a day at his desk, staring at a computer, he fancied a walk in the fresh air. Well, almost fresh air. A heron laboured overhead. The return of bird life meant that the government's attempts to clean up the river must finally be bearing fruit. You wouldn't want to fall in, though.

One developer had thought it a good idea to convert the

whole side of his gold-mirrored edifice into a giant LED screen. The sun was still setting in a pinkish glow over the Bund, but the 40-storey high, pixilated advertising was already declaring "I heart SH". As the boat passed mid-river, he could make out the old clock tower above the Customs House, which showed that it was almost VI o'clock. Plenty of time. He opened his briefcase to double-check that he had brought his invitation. The title of this evening's talk, to be held above the Prada showroom, was "America against itself". He doubted there would be many Americans there. He would mingle with the assembled apparatchiks and gather what intelligence he could.

The sound of the engines suddenly cut, as the pilot used the speed of the current to slew around and approach the landing-stage side-on. There were more people waiting on this bank. They pressed up against the bars of the gate impatient for the current load to dis-embark, passengers who had just come from where they wanted to go. As a ferry veteran, he knew where the door would start to open, so was first off, striding towards his date with dialectics and, hopefully, a large glass of red wine.

26

JUNE 1900

Act One: Besieged

(The sound of Chinese trumpets. Shouts of "Sha! Sha! Sha!" Sporadic shooting)

Morrison: Hey, you! What the hell are you doing?! Keep your head down there. Oh, Sir Robert. Sorry. I didn't see it was you. If you sit here you'll be fine. They are shooting high and wild.

Hart: I'm so sorry, Morrison.

Morrison: What are you doing out here? I thought all the high heid yins were in session at the Spanish Legation?

Hart: I stepped out. For a walk. Not that you can walk more than 100 paces in any direction now. My presence seemed to make their Excellencies…uneasy.

Morrison: It is because they are idiots. Your departure will have substantially reduced the average intelligence in the room. Not to mention all your years of experience as "Inspector General of Imperial Customs". Are all the ministers there?

Hart: Yes, all 11, sorry I mean 10, after what happened to poor Sugiyama-san. They've all received the same message from the Tsungli Yamen. The same ultimatum. All foreigners should leave the Legations within 24 hours for Tianjin, guarded along the way by Imperial troops.

Morrison: That would be the same Imperial troops who are allowing the Boxers to take pot shots at us? I don't imagine that debate will take very long.

Hart: Oh, I would not be so sure. Some of the ministers seem keen on a quick exit…

Morrison: Let me guess. Pichon will be one of them. "*Nous sommes perdu. Nous sommes finit.*"

Hart: That's actually a pretty good impression. Also the American, Conger.

Morrison: No! You surprise me.

Hart: Sir Claude is sitting on the fence, as usual, and has not committed himself. At least he hadn't before I left the room.

Morrison: Committing the foreign community, including 200 women and children, to the "protection" of these thugs is one thing. What do they think is going to happen to the 3,000 converts packed into the legations when we leave? Do they want that on their conscience? Or is the instinct for self-preservation really so overwhelming?

Hart: The fate of the Chinese converts is certainly an issue. I know you helped rescue a large number from the Cathedral. But the decision is not as clear cut as you suggest. Before we were cut off, I got a letter away to Viceroy Li Hongzhang…

Morrison: The Great Satrap

Hart: Li has his faults, but he is experienced and knows better than anyone at Court how the West thinks. I told him that harming the Legations would bring down a terrible retribution on China. Unfortunately, Prince Duan and the "patriotic" faction have the upper hand at Court, but there must still be advisors urging caution, or we would not now be sitting here talking.

Morrison: The Boxers make a lot of noise, but they do not seem keen to face our guns.

Hart: It is not a want of bravery. We can field what, 500 or 600 able-bodied men to hold these buildings? Our defences are makeshift, at best, and ammunition limited. From up on the

Tartar Wall, you will have seen the numbers that surround us. Were they to rush us at all points, how long do you think we could hold out?

Morrison: Not long.

Hart: The point is that the Empress Dowager herself well remembers what happened 40 years ago when her late husband last provoked a foreign invasion. But neither does she want the Boxers to turn their anger on the Manchu court. So, we are an embarrassment. I believe every effort would be made to convey the foreigners safely to Tianjin. I agree it would be hard to protect the converts, but if they were part of the same convoy…

Morrison: Would you trust your own family to them? I would have thought an old soldier like Sir Claude would remember the Siege of Cawnpore, when the British community were promised safe conduct then butchered.

Hart: My family have long lived back in England, as you know. Hessie and the children. I often thought of going back, but the timing never seemed right. They are all grown up now.

Morrison: I was sorry to hear about your house. Did all your possessions go up in flames?

Hart: We were able to rescue some volumes of correspondence, about 70 or so. But most of what I have collected over the years went up in smoke. What I miss most is my violin. And the porous plasters for my Lumbago. Also it would have been nice if my billiards table could have survived.

Morrison: This must be even more galling for you than for the rest of us. You have devoted your life to this country – sacrificed so much. I heard the Empress Dowager refers to you as "*Women de Ha-te*", "Our Hart". And now, here you are, fresh meat for a massacre.

Hart: Not much meat left on these old bones. Still, if we are to die, I suppose Peking is as close to heaven as any other place.

I have been fortunate to have had the chance to do what I have done here, with the customs service, the post office, and all those lighthouses. Most of the time, of course, I was just trying to keep the tyres on the wheel.

Morrison: Personally, I think your biggest achievement was Beijing's first brass band.

Hart: They weren't so bad, were they? It would be sad to leave things unfinished. It makes me think of my friend "Chinese" Gordon, as was. "Gordon of Khartoum" as he became. I wonder how he felt, after all his work for the Sudanese, walking out to meet his death on the spears of the Mahdi. He was a brave man, if sometimes ill-advised.

Morrison: It's not great, being speared.

Hart: Yes, you have told me your New Guinea war story.

Morrison: And I have heard all your Gordon stories. Let's just hope we avoid his fate. It is now nearly nine. That's when the evening fusillade usually starts, so you might want to find some shelter. Perhaps you could check in on what the idiot circle has decided?

Hart: I think I would prefer to my bunk. Good night! I'll leave you with the Boxers whilst I resume my nightly battle with the mosquitoes and cockroaches.

Morrison: Wouldn't a ride out to the Fragrant Hills be nice. Or maybe a swim down at Beidahe. At least we can dream of escaping this stinking dungeon.

Act 2 The Court

*(Shouting in Chinese)*良光總督到了

Li: Your Majesty. Your humble servant kneels before you and begs audience.

Cixi: Please get up, Viceroy Li. You must be weary after your long journey North. A seat here for the Viceroy! Viceroy Li, please do not stand on ceremony. You have my permission to sit.

Li: Thank you, your Majesty. It has been a wearisome journey, and my knees…but the urgency of the matter which I wish to raise with your Majesty…

Cixi: You look tired. Please take your time. Have some tea. Does the scar hurt?

Li: That Japanese assassin certainly did not improve my looks, but it does not hurt, thank you for asking. It has been some time since that unfortunate episode. But once again we seem to find ourselves…

Cixi: I know why you have come. I know what you want to say. But it is too late. I know that you are a fine historian—top *jinshi* degree, *banxiu* at the Hanlin Academy—so you will be familiar with the Yellow Turban rebellion that hastened the demise of the Han Dynasty?

Li: Peasant rebellion. Folk cult with supposed magic powers. Colourful headwear. I see the similarities to the Boxers. But the Yellow Turbans did not win.

Cixi: You miss my point. If this rebellion were to be directed against us, the great Qing, it could be dangerous. By appearing to support them, I have directed their anger against the foreigners, who were becoming increasingly…demanding. If the Boxers can push out the foreign devils, all well and good. If not, then they are expendable and we will explain to the foreigners how we were misled by nefarious advisers, and how we will certainly give serious consideration to their reform proposals.

Li: The Boxers are not as well-organized or led as the Yellow Turbans, and their armaments are little better. The Yellow Turbans were not facing opponents with artillery, machine guns and dreadnoughts. When I made my long journey to England, at your command, I was taken to a review of the British navy at a place called Spithead. I believe I have a better understanding of what we are facing than Prince Duan or General Tung. Five years ago, before our disastrous war against Japan, I begged you to be patient, to bide your time until we could build up a reformed and strengthened army. I beg you now, your Majesty, to suppress the Boxers and protect the Legations.

Cixi: We cannot afford another civil war. I am an old woman, and my memory is failing. But the experience of the Taiping rebellion is as fresh in my memory as it must be in yours.

Li: What we cannot afford are more punitive reparations, which the foreigners will impose if you massacre their representatives here. You know that Hart is amongst the besieged?

Cixi: I was told. Of course, I would give strict instructions that his life be spared.

Li: Do you think, amidst the blood, guts and smoke of a massacre, your armed peasants will distinguish one foreigner from another? I heard that they burnt the Hanlin?

Cixi: Yes, that was unfortunate. It borders the British Legation on the North side, and the wind from was from the North so they thought they could set fire to…

Li: The burning of China's finest library by our own forces strikes me as more than a misfortune. *(Sound of fan being opened sharply).* I am sorry. Forgive me, I mis-spoke.

Cixi: You are forgiven. I am an old woman, and my power to control events has its limits, as you must know. I gave the Legations a way out—evacuation to the coast, guarded by my own troops—but they refused to take it.

Li: My information is that they might have gone along with your proposal, were it not for the shooting of the German minister on his way to discuss the matter. Another misfortune. General Yuan seemed to be making a reasonable show of suppressing the Boxers in Shandong before he was…stood down. Perhaps you could bring him to Beijing and…

Cixi: It is a matter of trust. Someone who knows of the Yellow Turbans will certainly recognize the name An Lu-shan, the over-mighty general who almost brought down the Tang

Li: You mean which is the greater danger? Allowing continuing chaos, which invites foreign invasion, or concentrating power in the hands of a military man?

Cixi: Men like Prince Duan and General Tung have their limitations, but I understand their motives, and can hope to direct them accordingly. But for Yuan Shih-kai…?

Li: The foreign powers already hold the Dagu forts. If you persist in the current course, they will be here before the end of August. It is a bitter pill, I understand, but much better to seek a compromise now.

Cixi: Thank you for your advice, Viceroy Li. I have listened and will consider your views. Whatever the outcome, I will doubtless have need of your services to deal with the foreigners. I heard that you met with the rebel Sun Yat-sen in Guangzhou.

Li: Your majesty has good information. I find it useful to keep a tab on what our "revolutionaries" are up to.

Cai: How did you find him?

Li: He seemed a nice young man. Well-spoken. A little earnest. A medical doctor, you know?

Cai: I mean how did you locate him. I have read that we briefly held him at our legation in London.

Li: he came in for a talk, quite voluntarily.

Cai: What did he want?

Li: Oh, the normal sort of thing—the World! Arms, money, support. As your agents will have reported, I sent him away empty-handed. But he merits watching. His type is a lot more dangerous to us than the farmers-with-spears that you are worrying about here.

Act 3 Repast

(Sound of cicadas, occasional shots continue throughout. Clock ticking. A door opens.)

Condit Smith: Welcome back, Ernest. Your shift was a long one. We were just tidying up, but we've saved you some dinner.

Hart: Polly surpassed herself this evening. Guess what we ate.

Morrison: Now, let me think carefully. Um, rice and horse.

Hart: *(sarcastic)* How on earth did you…?

Morrison: Lucky guess.

Hart: It was lucky that all the ponies were gathered in Beijing for the races just before this all blew up. But there is an additional element today….jam!

Morrison: Oh, our mess is clearly an establishment of considerable sophistication.

Hart: And Polly managed to acquire one of those brown loaves from the Hotel de Pekin for our breakfast.

Condit Smith: It is on the table, dear. I'll brew the tea.

Morrison: Thank you, Polly. What I wouldn't give for a vegetable. I now remember all those years scraping boiled cabbage to the side of my plate with shame.

Hart: How are the defences looking?

Morrison: *(Mouth full)* Pretty thin. But I must say, for a missionary, the Reverend Gamewell and his Fortification Committee have done a good job on the barricades. *(Sings, with Hart joining in after the first line)* "Onward Christian soldiers, marching as to war, with the cross of Jesus going on before." As a group, the missionaries have made a decent contribution.

Condit Smith: With one or two exceptions. Have you seen Nestergaard, the Norwegian, recently? He's getting worse. Always stalking around in his cassock and that battered top hat, mumbling at the ground.

Morrison: I won't hear a word against old Nestergaard. He helped to rescue my book collection.

Condit Smith: And poor old Father Dosio seems to have cracked under the strain. His hair has turned completely white.

(Silence, but for cicadas, clock, and sound of a shot)

Morrison: Anyway, the ladies have been doing a fine job sewing and filling sandbags. I don't think I have ever seen such colourful sandbags before. I wondered what had happened to the embassy's curtains. It has been instructive how the siege has brought out the best and worst in people. I am not at all surprised that Backhouse is shirking duty. "A thigh wound" he claims, but he seemed to move fast enough when he wanted to "save" some valuable books from the Hanlin fire. He is a decent translator, but I wouldn't trust him behind me holding a gun, so perhaps his "injury" is just as well.

Hart: And how is our rainbow coalition getting along?

Morrison: Well, the Russians aren't speaking to the British, and vice-versa, so we have stationed them as far away from each other as is possible in our tiny enclave. The British call the Americans "Damned Yankees" and the Americans call the British "Damned Lime-juicers", but mostly in jest. The Germans don't speak to anyone, especially the French, apart from taunting the Brits about the fiasco in South Africa. And the Japanese can't speak to anyone, even if they wanted to. The Italians have been placed where they'll do least harm.

I do have one example of successful international co-operation to report, however. We used "the International Gun" today. That rusting canon we discovered from the 1860 invasion was mounted on an Italian carriage, and uses surplus 9lb Russian shells. Every time it fired, my heart was in my mouth. But it did good work against the barricades that the Chinese are pushing towards the Suwangfu wall.

Hart: I have a lot of time for Colonel Shiba. I think he and his men have done an excellent job in holding Prince Su's palace. It is the most exposed part of the line.

Morrison: Agreed. Man for man, the Americans are better shots, so it is good that they are up on the Tartar Wall. But in terms of organization and tenacity, the Japanese take the prize. Ably supported by your boys, of course, Sir Robert. "The Customs Volunteers". I am so sorry about Oliphant. I know he was one of your favourites.

Hart: Yes. Such a talented young chap. First in the exam. Three years here.

Condit Smith: A good dancer as well. A real charmer.

Hart: A bullet in the abdomen is not a good way to go. At least his brother was with him at the end. How many are in the hospital now?

Morrison: Well, if we are using "hospital" to refer to the large hall at the back of the embassy, then about 50. Dr. Velde does his best with very little. In this heat the stench is quite something. I am glad I smoke.

Hart: We are all smokers now. Tobacco and alcohol seem to be the only things not in short supply.

Condit Smith: The worst is to see the babies. Grey, limp. Poor little mites. All we have for dysentery is rice water. The converts are down to eating dogs and tree bark. I save the few eggs that are smuggled in for mothers with babies, but…You should thank God for your horse and rice. I don't think even that will stretch beyond another week or so. I am down to my last four tins of beef and will have to cut the coffee ration soon.

Morrison: No! I am not sure I can survive this two-hours-on, four-hours-off routine without some coffee, however thin.

Hart: We must think ourselves lucky that the Legation quarter has so many wells.

Condit Smith: What I miss most is clean linen. Who wants to die in dirty old underwear.

Morrison: What does it matter what you are massacred in?

Hart: Morrison, that was uncalled for.

Condit Smith: Is there really no news from the outside? What's taking them so long? Surely they know our situation by now?

Morrison: Nothing from my side. Nothing posted on the Bell Tower. I fear none of the messengers we sent got through. It is 80 miles to the coast, after all, through territory infested with bandits. I would not be surprised if the foreign enclave in Tianjin is also under attack.

Hart: All I can do is read between the lines of the official pronouncements we are sent. There was clearly some glee amongst our enemies around the failure of Admiral Seymour's rescue attempt—or Admiral See-no-more, as he is now dubbed.

Morrison: My favourite official communication was the one to Ambassador Pinchon that he had won the Legion d'Honneur and his mother sends her love. And to the Italian Legation with commiserations that King Humbert had been assassinated by a lunatic.

Hart: Given the increasing intensity of attacks recently, I believe another allied force must be on its way.

Condit Smith: Well, I keep a small pistol with me. Just in case the worst happens.

Hart: Oh, Polly, let's hope it does not come to that. Let's hope that the Dowager Empress does not do anything rash. That is not the old Buddha's style.

Morrison: *(Silence, except for the sound of eating. Then "Ride of the Valkyries" on the piano)*. There goes von Bulow again. Dramatic bunch these Germans. He must think another attack is on its way. I better finish this haute cuisine quickly. *(Sound of Chinese bugles,* *screaming and a crash of gunfire).* And here they come.

Act 4 Outside the Walls

(Noise of enthusiastic eating)

Shao: Hey, Lao Wang, pass the spinach.

Wang: There you go, Xiao Shao. It's not bad is it?

Shao: *(speaking with mouth full)* No, not bad at all. Not as good as when you "found" that duck last week.

Wang: Someone loses a duck, and someone finds one. Happens all the time.

Shao: You always were good at that sort of thing, Lao Wang. Is there any more rice?

Wang: Don't call me "Lao Wang". You should call me Red Spear.

Shao: What? I've always called you "Old Wang", and you always called me "Little Shao", even though I'm taller than you now.

Wang: It is a matter of hierarchy. I am the squad senior, so you should call me Red Spear. Especially in front of the other men.

Shao: All right, "Red Spear" *(giggles).*

Wang: Are you sorry you joined?

Shao: No. Definitely not. Some of the guys go on about home and their mother's cooking. But my mother's cooking is rubbish. And back in Mulangou, with my parents, grandpa, married older brother and two sisters, you had to look sharp at meals, or you ended up hungry. Even in a good season, four *mu* of corn, vegetables and a few peach trees for a whole family isn't going to stretch far. Look where we are now. Who would have ever thought I would get to see Beijing?! It would be nice if they would pay us, like proper soldiers. But we have managed to "find" a few valuables on the way, eh? Remember that old chap outside Jinan, with the pretty daughters and the gold clock, yeh?

Wang: But the cause? Our cause is right? *"Fu qing mie yang!"* "Revive the Qing, annihilate the foreigners".

Shao: Oh *"Fu qing mie yang"*. Of course! Remember Old Gong in our village, that rotting fish bladder, always running off to his priest when there was a dispute. Remember? Well he got what was coming to him. And his precious "congregation".

Wang: Well, those who couldn't run fast enough, anyway.

Shao: That was when I discovered my supernatural powers. The way a true Boxer can tell a Christian because of the cross they can see on their forehead.

Wang: It doesn't count if you make it with your own knife.

Shao: *(chuckles).* Anyway, the foreign devils iron tracks and wires are messing up the *fengshui* and disturbing our ancestors' graves. It's just been one disaster after another ever since they arrived. And all the carters thrown out of work. No, the cause is good. Do you really think the foreigners drink menstrual blood?

Wang: Please, I'm still eating!

Shao: No, really. The cousin of a friend of mine was on one of their ships, and said it was full of barrels of pickled limbs! Human limbs!

Wang: Please. Lay off. We should have a decent feed tonight. I am not sure when we'll get the next meal.

Shao: Really? *(in a low voice)* You think the big push is tonight?

Wang: It's what I've heard. Since General Li was put in charge of the Northern armies, things have tightened up. You will take care of yourself won't you?

Shao: What do you mean?

Wang: Well, there's no need to be right at the front. You know what they say—the bird in front gets the buckshot.

Shao: *(offended)* I've proved myself. I can use a halberd. I have my talisman with the tiger's whisker. I'm not afraid!

Wang: I wasn't suggesting...It's just the foreigners still seem to have enough ammunition. All I'm saying is you need to be careful, especially of those machine guns. And I promised your mother…

Shao: They can't touch me.

Wang: Have you not been paying attention? Have you not seen all our men they've shot? All those corpses being eaten by pariah dogs in the street.

Shao: They just didn't practice hard enough. Didn't believe hard enough. If you could find me a rifle, that would help. One of those Mausers. Or, better still, one of those Mannlicher carbines the guards have got. Then I wouldn't need to get so close.

Wang: I'll see what I can find

(The distant sound of "Ride of the Valkyries" is heard).

Shao: What the fuck is that? They make good rifles, but foreign music is really weird! Tonight I am going to find whoever plays that shit and personally chop off his hands. They give me the creeps with their green eyes and white hair. The music must be some ritual thing. Like my initiation when I drank the *baijiu* with pig's blood. You haven't got any *baijiu* with you by any chance?

Wang: Well, I guess this is as good a time as any to finish off the flask. Here. Have a swig. *Ganbei*!

Shao: *Ganbei*, Red Spear.

Act 5 Obituary

Morrison *(reading)*: The London Times, 17th July 1900. "Massacre in Peking. The Europeans fought with calm courage to the end against overwhelming hordes of fanatical barbarians thirsting for their blood. They have died as we would have them die, fighting to the last for the helpless women and children who were to be butchered over their dead bodies. One shudders to think of the awful days and nights waiting for the help that never came, before the tragedy was finally consummated, and the last heroic remnants of Western civilization in the doomed city were engulfed beneath the overwhelming flood of Asiatic barbarism" Good stuff, don't you think?

Hart: Well, if you like that kind of thing. A little purple, for my taste. Also there's the small issue of it bearing absolutely no relation to the truth.

Morrison: I thought I'd find you up here, so I brought you a spare copy of the paper. It is not often that a man gets to read his own obituary. Look, look, here it is: "Sir Robert Hart.blah blah… soon acquired by sheer force of character and ability an amount of influence over the Central Government which no foreigner had ever possessed" Quite right. "All the dogged perseverance, the shrewd intelligence, and business-like capacity of a typical Ulsterman." Some type-casting there. "Generously prone to only seeing the better side of men." Well, that's nice. "Blah, blah limitless capacity for work, considerable ambition and love of power." Oh, that's a bit of a poke. "He had loved the people for whom and with whom he had worked. He had lived with them so long that he had assimilated in some respects their ways of thought." i.e. You'd gone native. "The guns with which the legation was battered were paid for with loans raised on the credit Sir Robert Hart had created." That's harsh. They can't have it all ways.

Hart: Let's see yours. *(Rustling of paper)* "No newspaper has ever had a more devoted, a more fearless and a more able servant. His career is characteristic of one of the best types of colonial Englishman." We are both type-cast, it seems.

Morrison: Look, there's more. "Official confirmation used only to limp in with halting steps two or three days later". That's one in the eye for the diplomats. And look here "Essentially modest and unassuming, yet at the same time resolute and virile." Oh, I like that "Resolute and virile". I think I'll frame it.

Hart: Enough, enough, Mr. Modesty. Hand it over. *(Sound of paper being folded).* After that kind of write-up they'll have to give you a raise. Not that you'll be short of cash, from what I heard. You've been taking part in the looting.

Morrison: Oh, there's some excellent value to be had. This morning, for just $2, a Sikh gentleman sold me a fine gold cloisonné clock and two chickens.

Hart: Aren't you even a little ashamed?

Morrison: Spoils of war. Hey, what are you doing?

Hart: Did they not teach you how to make paper darts at Geelong Grammar? I bet you I can hit the burnt-out temple down there. Wheee…

Morrison: Why should I stand aside and let the Germans and Japanese take it all. I heard the wife of our illustrious ambassador was last seen dispatching 97 chests of loot to the coast.

Hart: Oh, so close. If it had just flown a bit straighter…

Morrison: Are you really going to stay on, after what they did to you?

Hart: I am horribly hurt by all that has occurred, of course, but I do not want my career to end in failure. "*Finis coronat opus*". Just look down there. A thriving city made a desert, picked clean. They will need me more than ever now, to stop the Western powers doing to China what the foreign soldiers have done to the palaces of Beijing—with a little help from people who should know better. I will also be needed by the foreign powers, though they don't know it yet, to stop them drawing the wrong conclusion from this fiasco. The Chinese people are not the same as their leaders. They are industrious, law-abiding and polite. This huge country will be strong one day.

Morrison: And what of your family?

Hart: It is over 10 years since I saw Hessie and our children. I write every week, of course, but every now and then I do feel a spasm of loneliness.

Morrison: And what about your three older children by your previous…?

Hart: It is not a secret.

Morrison: Well, if a journalist knows about it, you can be sure of that.

Hart: I was a young man, alone in China, I took a Chinese wife. It is not so strange. Poor little Ayou. I had our children educated in England—Anna, Herbert and Arthur. Found them jobs, places. They all found themselves spouses—mostly unsuitable. Campbell in London keeps me up to date on their progress. I am not ashamed of it. Well, that's not quite right. I am ashamed of giving in to what society expected of me. Setting Ayou aside. Paying her off. Going back to find a nice, appropriate Irish wife. Hessie did her best—she was a good pianist you know—but in the end she could not bear it here. Some days I think the family now just look at me as a goldmine. Still, would I really be of more use to them living back in the Home Counties, when there is so much to do here? No, I'll wait on. My faith is great in time and that which shapes it to a perfect end.

Act 6: Epitaph

Narrator: the Dowager Empress fled Beijing in a mule cart five hours before foreign troops of the "Eight Army Alliance" entered the city on August 15th 1900. The first troops to enter were a Sikh regiment. Commander Gaslee's first words were recorded as "Thank God, men, here are two women alive". The siege had lasted 55 days and had resulted in 68 Westerners being killed and 159 wounded. Chinese casualties? They were never counted.

Li Hongzhang and Prince Ching negotiated peace terms with the Eight Foreign Powers and signed the Boxer Protocol in September 1901. Some of those courtiers adjudged most to blame were executed, others banished. There were no territorial concessions, though the Dagu forts were disassembled. However, reparations of 450 million taels were to be paid over 39 years. Of this, 29% was owed to Russia, 20% to Germany and so forth. Only the United States of America declined to take a slice of the pie.

Hart stayed on. His house was rebuilt by the end of 1901. He pushed through an increase in the import tariff from 3.17% to 5% and imposed higher taxes on items used mostly by the foreign community. His Customs Service took over internal tariffs. In total this raised an additional 20 million taels income per annum. You could say that, to some extent, he got foreigners to pay their own reparations. He was awarded with the order of the peacock's feather by the Dowager Empress.

Cixi: For decades Your Excellency has lent your talents to a land that is not your own, and today your sincere devotion to it is clear to all. I cannot be more appreciative.

Narrator: Sir Robert left his post in the same year in which Cixi died. His successor arrived to find a note pinned over his desk "7am, 13th April 1908. Gone Out. R.H." He died of pneumonia in Marlow Buckinghamshire in 1911, the same year in which the Great Qing dynasty, which he had served so effectively for nearly 50 years, expired. A fine bronze statue of him was erected on the Bund in Shanghai in 1912, where it stood until it was destroyed in 1942 by the next set of invaders.

(Sounds of volley fire, as over a grave).

27

Off My Head

People go to a lot of trouble to get off their heads. They are willing to spend a lot to forget their particular problems. Alcohol is popular, though it seems, from the number of zero-alcohol beverages filling supermarket shelves, that its social acceptability may be declining. For much of my career alcohol was not only acceptable but also, in certain circumstances—at the business dinner, after the match—almost obligatory. Some like to lose themselves in music, or in support of a sports team. For the mindful, there is yoga and meditation. For the determined there is a range of opiates and other harder narcotics.

I don't need any of this. Now I get off my head for free, on average, once a day. As a man who likes to be in control, I have never been terribly keen on chemical evasion. But I have epilepsy. Fortunately, it is not the falling-down-frothing-at-the-mouth variety. It is just that, for a few seconds, I am not there. There is a metallic taste in the mouth, then I am not me, but an actor in someone else's life; truly a stranger in a strange land.

When this started, in my 50's, I did not know what it was. I called them "attacks" and searched for a trigger. Some allergy? A sensitivity to flashing lights? Perhaps it was linked to anxiety or tiredness? No explanation quite seemed to fit. I remember marking times in my diary to see if there was a pattern.

Because of the nature of my life, the attacks tend to happen when I am alone, sitting at a desk, reading or writing. In this context it is just mildly disconcerting. Even when I am with others, as long as I am not talking at the time, or required to do something, it takes someone who knows to spot the signs—a sudden stiffening, face turning grey. It is only when I am in mid-conversation that it is embarrassing. A normally fluent man suddenly falters, looks confused, needs to clutch onto a chair for support. It is also not helpful when I am driving, but I don't do much of that. I have only been beeped once when failing to move away on a green light.

In some way it was a relief when I found the cause. A brain tumour. After seeing the problem, my wife, over-riding my it-will-be-fine, stiff-upper-lip excuses, booked me in for an MRI brain scan. Of course, discovering one has a brain tumour is not great—it certainly concentrates the mind on one's own mortality. But at least the doctor allowed me to put a name to it: "absence epilepsy". It is also only a small tumour, in the right Hippocampus, and seemingly benign. The Taiwanese doctor trying to reassure me, whilst glancing through the rest of my health report, said: "Don't worry about it. You will probably die of something else first." I am prescribed pills, which do not seem to make much of a difference.

During the attacks, the overwhelming sensation, which might surprise you, is one of loneliness. If I am not me, then who the hell am I?

About the Author

Born in Yorkshire, Chris has spent over 30 years working in Asia. He studied Chinese at Oxford University and Japanese at Sheffield University. He sold soap for Procter & Gamble in Newcastle, traded metals in Beijing, Shanghai and Sydney and was a financial analyst in Tokyo, Taipei, Hong Kong, Edinburgh and Shanghai. His previous works include "A Decent Bottle of Wine in China", "The Barter Trade" and "Before the Wall". Chris is married with four children and lives in London.

Made in United States
North Haven, CT
05 December 2025

83645272R00094